Sweet Peppers - Sour Grapes and Wild Flowers

By

Mary F. Carter

This book is a work of fiction. Places, events, and situations in this story are purely fictional. Any resemblance to actual persons, living or dead, is coincidental.

© 2002 by Mary Flowers Carter. All rights reserved.

No part of this book may be reproduced, stored in a retrieval system, or transmitted by any means, electronic, mechanical, photocopying, recording, or otherwise, without written permission from the author.

ISBN: 1-4033-8847-4 (e-book)
ISBN: 1-4033-8848-2 (Paperback)

Library of Congress Control Number: 2002096074

This book is printed on acid free paper.

Printed in the United States of America
Bloomington, IN

1stBooks - rev. 08/04/03

Acknowledgements

I have been truly fortunate to have my husband, Charles Carter, my two daughters, Daphne Carter Wright and Dr. Charletta Carter, and my son-in-law, Michael Wright as my staunch supporters. They believed in me more than I believed in myself. Their encouragement kept me on task when the novel was still fragile and unpredictable.

I extend heartfelt thanks to my church friends whose love and support have been invaluable. Special thanks to Mrs. Lavonne Reedus and Mrs. J. Moffett Walker.

Also, I thank God for giving me the wisdom to write this novel.

Dedication

This novel is dedicated to my two grandchildren, Maryssa Kathleen Wright and Charles Michael Wright.

Prologue

It was in September 1999 when Sarah and Tom were swerving back and forth as the wild fierce wind was bashing and heaving their new Oldsmobile as if it were made of paper. Branches were being ripped and splintered from trees and tossed in all directions. The palpitation of rain on the windshield seemed to be so powerful that they thought that it would shatter the windshield. Blinded by the debris, Tom tried mercifully to hang on to the steering wheel with great anticipation for a future. Sarah started crying as she always did when she felt that there was trouble. They were well aware that in their hometown of Kingston, Virginia, the powerful forcible hurricane, Betsy, was roughly at play with all its drama.

As the potent storm plowed across the eastern half of the nation, it unraveled the top from their tan convertible Oldsmobile. The hemp canvas, hazardously, dangled on the rear of the car making a horrendous sound. Suddenly, with another strong blast of wind, the canvas unleashed itself and floated dangerously down the highway. Cringing with fear, Sarah's deprivation of consciousness impeded her ability to think, and Sarah found it impossible to pray. Therefore, she ducked down and stooped in a servile position on the floor of the car. The close quarters seemed to have induced asphyxia, which made her feel that her head was made of a block of ice, and her extremities had vanished. To say the least, she felt that there was no hope against hope.

Consumed by desperation to control the car, Tom was not afforded the opportunity to crouch to safety. Holding on with intensity, he fought to maneuver the car. As his struggle seemed to somewhat lessen, the vehement storm ripped the door from the driver's side of their car. With determination to defeat this obstacle, he plastered his hands and body against the steering wheel. He felt that at any moment, the ferocious wind was going to thrust him out of his seat and propel him into the air.

Early on, Tom had let up on the accelerator and had an inclination to come to a halt, but feared a tail end collision. As he peeped out the opening, to his amazement, there were no shoulders constructed at this particular section of the highway. During his contemplation, a savagely fierce gust of wind rushed under the car and propelled it into trees where it was suspended momentarily. Branches and limbs began snapping and cracking. The sounds were terrifying, yet it was music to Sarah's ears, because being able to perceive by ear was an indicant that she was still alive.

Just as Sarah was feeling a twinge of animation, a forklike branch splintered across her face. The spurting of blood blinded her as the car landed in a muddy creek. The distressing sensation of the blow had almost numbed her just as she was retrieving some consciousness from the prior panicky situation. As she peered through gore, she observed Tom as he was still gripping the steering wheel. He was sitting motionless and staring straight ahead. Sarah muttered, "Tom, Tom, Tom!!!"

Tom, painstakingly, turned his head that was covered with blood, but he managed to utter, "Yes-es Sa-rah."

Sarah realized that he was in a mental torpor, and he needed some kind of jolt to regain some normalcy. While still in her servile position with a shroud of muddy water up to her waistline, she jostled his leg with her elbow. Gradually, he released the steering wheel, and his body seemed to become less tense and rigid.

Numerous groups of organisms adhered to the surface of the muddy water. As the grimy filthy water was moving upward, it emitted a strong offensive smell that caused Tom and Sarah to become breathless. Suddenly, Sarah became nauseous and began to regurgitate. The spew made the stench even more apparent to the both of them.

Observing Sarah eject the content from her stomach, Tom began to try to mobilize himself. As he shifted his position, the car began to gradually descend even more. Encountering the downward movement, they decided to become motionless for a while. The petrified two sat as if they were paralyzed, for they only moved their eyeballs. The four eyes resembled saucers with four black balls rolling around in them.

Just then, a cheery slimy brown frog leaped into the back seat as if it were soliciting a ride. It frolicked around in the back while it was making its froggy noise. The mud splattered all over the back of Tom and Sarah's heads, for they felt as if they were receiving their second christening. Just as the frog was about to give Tom the heebie-jeebies, it leaped on the back of the car and sprang into the muddy water.

Tom was about to make a suggestion when another pestersome visitor encroached upon them. The seemly lovely brownish bird had been in the proximity for some time. It flew back and forth overhead until it landed on Sarah's head. Arrogantly, it stood there while it cheerfully went, "Chirp, Chirp, Chirp!" It began moving its feet as if it were trying to prepare for a nest in her weaved hair. Naturally, Tom wanted to assist Sarah, but he was apprehensive about movement. Continuing his statuelike position, he partially separated his lips and through his teeth, he muttered, "Shoo, Shoo, Shoo." The bird ignored him and continued its constant and earnest effort to accomplish the task that it had undertaken. Becoming aware of the bird's stubbornness, Sarah slowly moved her arm upward without moving her body; she gently brushed the bird from her head. As her fingers touched her head, she gasped, "Oh My God! That bird used my head for a toilet!" As the words exuded from her mouth, she observed Tom staring in one direction. From his expression, she discerned imminent danger. Calmly, she eased up on the seat where she was somewhat out of the unpleasant mess. Now the slime was just below her knees. Apprehensively, she moved her head to look in the same direction as Tom. Her eyes perceived a snake swimming in front of the car, and one was even crawling on the front of the car. Tom finally vocalized to Sarah, "We might end up dead or alive, but we are **not** going to sit here motionless! At this point, we must fight for our lives! Sarah, you must be willing to do what I ask you to do. Are you willing?"

By this time, Sarah was shuddering convulsively from the cool air and also from the fright of the snakes that confronted them. Consequently, all the vocalizing that Tom was doing sounded like murky chatter. Probing in her unsound mind for words, she decided that she would not question his intentions; she would just follow orders. Muttering in a low, faint voice, Sarah answered Tom, "I will follow your orders."

Chapter I

Before the Arrival

For the saga began sometime ago in Kingston, Virginia when Tom Best first spoke to the Pastor Carl Levi on the telephone in the month of February 1999.

"Yes," stated Tom. "That sounds great." ... " Of Course."... "That's the way I think we all feel here at Saint Luke."..."We would be delighted."... "Great! Great! Great!" ... "How wonderful!" ... "I'll meet you at eleven o'clock at the train station." "Bye, Bye, and have a good night, and I'll see you Thursday morning."

With a sigh of relief, Tom swiftly hung up the telephone. His face reflected a sense of confidence and assurance. Through his glowing smile, he happily turned to Sarah and announced, "Honey, The Pastor Carl Levi seems to be just what we are looking for at St. Luke Church, for he seems to have practical theological views on life. On Thursday, I'll meet him and his family at the train station, and on Sunday, we will have a very jubilant celebration at the church."

Laboriously swallowing a sip of her herbal tea, Sarah smiled and gave Tom a big hug as she declared, "We have been praying and looking forward to this day, and this day has finally come, February 2nd."

The late Pastor Daniel Trombone had served at St. Luke for thirty years. He was married to Betty, and she gave birth to five children. When hundreds of both African-American and Native-American children were being bypassed and not being adopted, the Trombones became an interracial family in the adoption of Candice and Freddy. With the saving Gospel of Jesus Christ at the heart of his ministry, Pastor Trombone remained active in the areas of mission and social ministry concerns. In both professional and personal roles Pastor Trombone proved himself an extraordinary individual. The congregation at St. Luke was grateful to God for His providence.

The vacancy occurred at St. Luke six years ago. During this duration of time, the president of the Board of Directors was in consultation with Pastor John Elbert, Kingston Circuit Counselor, requesting names of nominees from the President of the District, Pastor Neal Gore. From time to time, many official lists were submitted to the Board of Directors; however, nothing materialized until about a month ago. Subsequently, a special General Voters' Assembly meeting was conducted to select a pastor from a list of three people whom no one in the congregation had ever seen or heard-of. Scanty information was submitted on each candidate. The members proceeded by secret ballots to elect a pastor. Notwithstanding, Carl Levi was divorced and had remarried, he received the majority of the votes, and currently, the obscure Carl Levi was progressing toward Kingston, Virginia.

Kingston had real beautiful surroundings for all of the members of St. Luke's Church. There were small animals such as rabbits and squirrels that were like little kinfolks. They were looked on as friends and playmates. The community was comprised of admirable elegant birds and butterflies with marvelous varied colors. Entrenched in some of the vacant areas were flowers that were brighter than colored balloons and grass as green as brilliant emerald. There were trees that towered like colossal statues. Their branches spread over the homes with a warm embrace.

St. Luke Church began with a small building some years ago. Under Pastor Trombone's administration, the church was replaced to be commensurable with the community. Over the years all of its authenticity had been preserved, and the maintenance had been an important consideration. The building always complied with the current standards of safety, structural stability, and energy conservation.

Across the community, word spread that the prospective Pastor Levi would be arriving on the early train Thursday morning.

Holly Holland, a staunch member of the church, was overjoyed about the news; however, her husband, James felt that this might be another person that would try to save his soul, and he wanted no parts of Pastor Levi or any other Pastor. Holly occupied her day attending her flower garden and house, for she was an immaculate housekeeper. One warm sunny evening, Holly was attending her flowers by the fence when Nellie Gray appeared from her garden and with excitement in her voice, she yelled, "Did you hear about the new minister? I was about to think that we were not going to get one in my life time."

"You know prayers change things in anybody's life time," stated Holly. "Tom will be picking him up from the train station on Thursday, for I am wondering what he looks like."

"I heard that he is a premature balding middle age man. I wonder if he's married?" asked the inquisitive Nellie.

Holly turned around, put her hands on her hips, shook her head and looked straight into Nellie's eyes as she spoke very slowly, "Nellie, he is not looking for a wife. I heard that he is very devoted to his wife and two children. You'll just have to look some other place."

"I'll look any place I please and …", but before she could finish, she saw James Holland, Holly's husband, coming up the driveway, and he wasn't walking very straight.

James relished the idea of patronizing the bar, so many evenings, he would request that Sammy, who was the maintenance supervisor for St. Luke, let him off at the bar, and he would walk home later. Reluctantly, Sammy would obey; however, he had a great concern for James' family because of James' drinking problem. This particular evening, James staggered home in a drunken stupor. As he dragged himself into the house, Holly rushed over to the side of the yard and got a piece of a bush, which was known as a switch. She swooped into the house behind James. Flopping down on the divan, she snatched James across her lap thrashing him across his legs, back and arms. As she switched him, she repeated in rap fashion, "Why- did – you- come -home -drunk? Don't- come -home –drunk- again. Do- you- hear- me?"

James kicked and lamented, "Don't know why! Didn't have that much!" She didn't listen to him, for she continued switching him until exhaustion overcame her. Swollen welts on his legs, arms and back, James wept throughout dinner. With a demanding voice, Holly said, "If you don't shut up, I'll give you more," and she squinted her eyes.

For the most part, the three children in the Holland family, Kathy Lou, Annie Mae and Billy, were as quiet as church mice. But recently, Kathy Lou, who was an adult now and in her second year at the community college, had feelings of frustration. Those feelings were forcing her to play an increasingly vocal role. Profoundly shaken by this unorthodox activity in the household, Kathy heard a voice from her mouth, "Mom, you have no right to lay a hand on Dad!"

"Well, he has no right to come home drunk. If he is going to act like a child, I'll treat him like a child." Holly strutted out of the room, and from the bedroom, she shouted, "I'll do the same to you if you don't shut your trap. Good sense should tell you to be quiet."

In an undertone, Kathy murmured, "Wrong! Wrong! Wrong!" All the time Kathy knew that she was treading dangerous waters when she talked back to her mother or spoke up for her father. Holly could and would switch the children when she felt that they were in need.

There was so much commotion in the house that no one was aware that Tom Best was coming up the walk. Holly ran to the door. "Good evening, Tom, how are you doing? This afternoon I was just discussing with Nellie about our new Pastor and his family."

"Yes", Tom said, "I...."

"We should have a dinner for them or maybe a welcome program of some kind, and you know it is so wonderful to know that we are getting a minister." Holly chattered on and on as Tom tried to speak again. "I think....."

"We are truly thankful that this is happening to us – a minister – my it's been a long time," Holly continued on and on as she blocked the doorway to her house.

"Good day," was all that Tom could squeeze in as he turned and walked to his car. Just as he was about to drive away, Dr. Hue Dawson drove up in his new Cadillac. "Good Evening, Doc, you do know that our new minister will be arriving in town on Thursday morning?"

Dr. Dawson stood tall and straight in a debonair manner, for he was quite impressive with his brown skin and masculine appearance. He was well proportioned, personable and good-looking with his neatly shaven head. He was highly in demand as a doctor, and almost every lady in the congregation who laid eyes on him inhaled and exhaled simultaneously. It was well known that he consorted with some of the lady members. The church had rules, and from that aspect, Hue knew that he was like a juggler dancing on the highest trapeze, and he was down right daringly walking a tightrope high above the earth. Yet the thrill was so transcendent that he felt pious rather than satanic. A certain amount of euphoria was obtained when Hue had successfully completed a rendezvous with one of the church ladies.

With his fair-spoken voice, Hue answered, "Good Evening, Tom. I heard the good news. Oh, how blessed we are."

"Yes, I will have the great privilege of picking him up at the train station on Thursday," Tom proudly announced.

"Will he be on the 9:00 or the 11:00 train?"

"Oh, he'll be on the 11:00, and he will have his whole family with him."

"Whole family?" Hue looked in amazement. "Where are they going to stay?".

Feeling a little squeamish, Tom shuffled his body around, as he searched for words to discuss this delicate matter. He had planned to approach Hue about this earlier in the week, but he was very reluctant. Scratching his head, Tom began the most appropriate way he knew how… " Well, Hue, it seems that- that Pastor Levi will be making contact with a contractor for the construction of a house right away, and –and if- if you could see fit, the family could spend that short time at your house."

"Well- ur- maybe- ur, I guess- so. I do have the whole house to myself since Jonnie Mae passed away," Hue stuttered with a feeling of apprehension.

"Are you sure, Hue?"

"Well –I- guess I'm sure. I- ur - really can't think of any other place for them to stay."

"Thank you! Thank you! But we'll discuss it further before they arrive." Then the two men shook hands as they parted.

As Tom drove home, his mind was racing fifty miles a minutes with fifty million questions running through his head: *"What will the minister look like? How will he and the family like staying with Hue for a while? Would the minister like the congregation? On the other hand, would the congregation like the minister? Etc, etc."*

After parking his car, Tom quietly went into the house. He found that Sarah had gone to bed early and was fast asleep, for she had had a busy day with her kindergarten class at Kingston Elementary School. He thought that she looked so dainty and beautiful as his sexual desires roused. As he scrutinized her vibrating body as she slept, he started to reminisce about the past.

It was a crisp winter day as he was on his way home from Honolulu, Hawaii where he was stationed in the Navy. Wanting to make it an adventurous trip, he thought that he might take a plane to New York, spend some time with his cousin, and then take a bus to Kingston, Virginia.

When he arrived in New York City, the snow was falling softly, glittering like pearls. The icicles were hanging like twinkling diamonds and sparkling clean crystal. He hailed a taxicab and handed him the address on 72nd Street in Manhattan. The cab was paid and tipped generously.

Wide-eyed and bushy tailed, he marched up to the apartment's outside door, which stood wide open. "No security!" he thought. His starry eyes skimmed the names on the mailboxes until his eyes caught, "Tammi Smythe". He remembered that it was "Tammy Lee Smith" back in Virginia. He had not seen his cousin for years, so he was somewhat hesitant to ring the bell. With his heart palpitating, his benumbed frigid fingers gently pushed the arduous doorbell. From the speaker came an incoherent voice, "Wh-o-o 'sit?"

"Tom- Tom Best," he answered, and he straightened his clothes and adjusted his duffel bag that was hanging over his shoulder.

"Who's To-o-m B-est?" came another stuttering voice from the speaker.

"Your cousin from Kingston, Virginia. Didn't you get my letter?"

"Oh! Yes! Today i- s the day! J-u-st a minute!"

It seemed to have taken a year and day before he heard an almost inaudible buzzer. With considerable skepticism, he opened the door and trudged up five flights of stairs.

His cousin, Tammy, stood provocatively in the doorway with a small shapely body clothed in a bra and some panties, and there was loud music playing in the background. "Come on in, boy! You look g-o-o-d! You one of those hotshot soldiers now, huh?"

Just as he began to put his duffel bag on the floor, his eyes glanced over at the couch, and there sat a young man naked as a jaybird. He reminded him of a sly fox grinning and exposing his pearly white teeth. "Hi, I'm Mike. And you must be Tammy's cousin."

"Yes, I- I- I am Tom – Tom," and as he spoke, he tried to ignore the unclad being.

Mike executed a sense of melodrama as he elevated himself on his brown skinny legs, "Oh, You- her aunt's boy that's in the Navy."

"Yes-s-s," he stammered. With his sweaty palms and palpitating heart, he quickly scooped up his duffel bag and raced out the door trying to escape one of the most uncomfortable predicaments of his lifetime.

After walking for a while, discomfiture and numbness were gradually dissipating, and his head was clearing. That instant he knew he must find the bus station, so that he could continue his trip to Kingston, Virginia. A cab was just zooming by and noticed that he was thumbing for a ride. Making a swift U-turn, the driver returned. He hopped in, gasping for breath, as he requested the driver to take him to the bus station.

Upon his arrival at the station, he fumbled and scuffled to get himself and his duffel bag out of the cab; however, it seemed that his duffel bag was deliberately trying to defy him. All at once the bag unleashed itself causing him to slip on the ice and slide under the cab. Recapturing his composure, he paid the driver and hurried into the station. Emerging into the doorway, his eyes glimpsed a young lady who was a vision of feminine beauty sitting over on a seat near the window. With admiration, he noticed that she was so engrossed in reading a book that nothing seemed to distract her. Several times, he purposely pranced by her before she looked up and smiled. As he gave her his most charming smile, he proudly strutted over and introduced himself. "Hello there, I'm Tom."

"I'm Sarah."

"Sorry to interrupt your reading," he enunciated very carefully. Proceeding to sit, he asked, "May I sit down?"

As Sarah closed her book, she spoke in her very soft lovely voice, "Sure!"

When he was seated, she asked, "Where are you headed?"

"I'm on my way to Kingston, Virginia, he disclosed. "Where are you headed?"

With exhilaration, Sarah enounced, "I'm on my way to Oxford, Virginia. We seem to going to almost the same place."

"I grew up in Kingston," he smiled with his pearly white teeth.

Flushing with happiness and disbelief, Sarah blissfully stated, "And I grew up in Oxford. What a coincident?"

He was trying not be too inquisitive, but before he knew it, he asked, "What are you doing in New York?"

Sarah was so excited about the fact that Tom desired to know all about her, and she was ready to tell him everything, "I spent some time with friends and relatives; however, I am a junior at Morgan State University."

Wanting to know more, Tom asked, "What is your major?"

"Elementary Education," Sarah cheerfully answered.

Just then, the Greyhound bus call was made, and he and Sarah made their way to the bus and sat next to each other……

Snapping back to reality, Tom realized that in actuality, he should be getting dressed for bed. After all tomorrow was a workday. After quickly disrobing, he searched for his pajamas. Unsuccessful, he decided to sleep in the buff. Moving close to Sarah and wrapping his arms around her seductively, he was quickly aroused; however, he remembered their agreement, "Never wake the partner from a sound restful sleep." He rolled over as he repeated, "Thank you, God, for all things and especially my charming, good-natured Christian wife and my two beautiful daughters who are many miles away in college, Amen." Peacefully, he harmonized his snore with Sarah's.

Chapter II

The Arrival

On Thursday morning the radiant sun rose on a perfect landscape of the finale of winter splendor and was shining through the window. As quietness embraced Sarah, she rolled over and reached for Tom; however, he was up, and she could smell the fresh breakfast cooking in the kitchen. "What a beautiful day," she thought, as she sprang from her bed and rushed down to breakfast.

On Wednesday night, Tom had gone over to Hue's house to insure that the Pastor had temporary residence. "Good morning, sweetie," Sarah whispered as she went over and kissed Tom on the cheek.

"Mornin, Mornin, how are you?"... as Tom imitated her country relatives.

"What time did you get home last night?"

"It was not very late, for Hue and I had much to discuss about the minister."

"Did you get it all straightened out?"

"Yes, let's hurry because we will have to be at the train station by 11:00."

Sarah was very inquisitive about the matter, but she dared not ask about it because Tom tended to be confidential about the business of his organizations.

Tom and Sarah ate breakfast in silence, as Sarah could sense that Tom's mind was on overload.

After breakfast, Sarah quickly cleared the dishes, cleaned the table, and they both got dressed for their trip to the train station.

As the two drove to the station, the cooler temperature of the early morning had begun to climb to the high 60's, as the sun rose in the pastel sky. The leaves on the trees seemed undisturbed, for they seem to be reminiscing about the late, Pastor Trombone. They seemed to have been thinking the same as Tom and Sarah, "Oh! How we miss Pastor Trombone. He was such a committed philanthropist, for his leadership went far beyond the church. Showing fortitude and endurance, he walked miles to support the spread of the Gospel. As he walked, he did clean-ups. Many times he would come home with bags of debris and garbage that he had gathered by the roadside. The members could see true missionary work as he led them in assisting those who suffered from natural or man-made catastrophes. The definition of Christianity was clearly taught by Pastor Trombone. There is certainly a vacancy in the hearts of St. Luke members. Today, we hope that this pastor would fill the void."

Jolting back to present time and trying not to reveal his apprehension, Tom finally said, "We pray that God will order our day because we don't know what to expect." Sarah was always a great witness, for she curiously looked at Tom and stated, "I am sure that God's word will prepare and sustain us as we face these unknown choices ahead." After a somewhat strained ride to the station, the two arrived at the parking lot just as the rude rumbling of the train began to intrude on the quietness that was just experienced in Kingston.

With ponderous thoughts, the two exited from the car and hustled through the parking lot, so that they would be at the train's door to welcome the new Pastor and his family. They stationed themselves by the tracks and stood soldierly side-by-side until the train came to a complete stop.

Several travelers departed the car until to their wandering eyes there appeared from the door of the train a gauche, blonde, blue-eyed guy that had the appearance of a vagabond. He wore faded threadbare blue jeans that hovered above his ankles while displaying his dingy white socks. His attire also included a grayish-stretched fuzzy sweater and gym shoes that looked ancient. In his hand was a dilapidated suitcase. Behind him came an impeccable dressed lady with elegantly braided hair, smooth brown skin and voluptuous cherry lips. She was carrying a brand new Gucci leather suitcase and was dressed in a 'Jones of New York' red linen suit with shoes and purse to match.

Tom and Sarah looked at the incomparable people and rejected any notion that those were the prospective church leaders. With tenacity, they stood and waited for another couple to depart, but there wasn't anyone else on the train other than two children. The two children sprang from the train as if they had been let out of prison.

Sweet Peppers-Sour Grapes & Wild Flowers

While Tom's eyes were still scrutinizing the door of the train's car, the conductor closed the door and waved good-bye to Tom and Sarah. Then the train went chug, chug, chugging along.

Suddenly, Tom began speculating curiously about the Levi's accurate arrival time. As he stood in perplexity, the oddly dressed man sauntered over to him, "How are you? You must be Mr. Tom Best."

Tom attempted to disguise his astonishment, "Yes, I am Tom, and you are…"

"Pastor Carl Levi," voiced the oddly dressed man.

Tom extended his hand, and Pastor Levi momentarily hesitated; then he gave Tom the weakest handshake that Tom had ever witnessed. Carl Levi stared and said, "This is my wife, Clara Levi, and those are my children, Kate and Kirk. They are twins with Kate being the older."

The children were chasing and hitting each other. Carl and Clara ignored their behavior.

Sarah glared and gawked at them with her starry brown eyes until Tom hunched her. "This is my wife Sarah."

"Hi - hi, ho-ow are you?" Sarah stammered. "We'll get your luggage."

"We have our luggage," Clara announced in a sophisticated voice.

Inconspicuously, Sarah scrutinized the Levi family, and she thought, *"Carl resembles a nomad, but sounds a little egotistical, while Clara resembles an Egyptian queen, but also seems a little haughty."*

It was almost impossible for Tom, Pastor Levi and Clara to talk, for the children were circling them and playing tag with their small suitcases. It was obvious that the children were out of control. Tom was trying to explain the living arrangements that he had so thoughtfully made with Dr. Hue Dawson.

Firmly planting his feet on the ground to bolster himself so as to prevent an accident that might happen from the children's pulling and tugging, Tom began, "You and the family will be living with Dr. Hue Dawson until you have your house completed. You stated on the phone that you wanted to begin building a new home as soon as you arrived, and it seems that you have already made arrangements to purchase a lot."

With a very strange voice, Carl rattled, "Yes, I would like for things to begin right away. I have considered a lot on Cherry Street. A few contractors have been recommended; however, I would like to consider your recommendations first. Do you know of any good, or I should say excellent contractors?"

"Yes, in fact, we have a couple of excellent contractors who belong to our church. You will have an opportunity to meet them."

Standing erect on her smooth delicate brown beautiful legs, Clara chimed in, "Oh, I'm so excited about being here, and to think that I'm getting a new home."

All of a sudden, Tom announced, "Well, you have your luggage. If you'll just follow me, we will find the car." The Bests and the Levis proceeded to the car, climbed in and were on their way to Hue's house.

Driving cautiously across the plateau to specious acres of wooded land, an awesome two-story brick house stood with a circular driveway, a picnic area with built-in grills, an indoor swimming pool and a three-car garage. The house was graced with many exquisite details. Vaulted ceiling complemented the living and great room. Ceramic tile in the entranceway introduced the walnut staircase, and marble was utilized through out the kitchen and breakfast nook. All of the brass fixtures were carefully selected. Some of the rooms were endowed with carpets that were made from fleece that was specially ordered from a custom weaving house specializing in hand woven carpets. The breakfast nook overlooked the picnic area that was surrounded with a beautiful colorful garden.

The late Jonnie Mae, Hue's wife, had hired a topnotch designer and retained her until the perfect selections of furniture, wall hangings and accent pieces were to her satisfaction. She was passionately devoted to this serene establishment. Gracefully, she managed the estate with several domestic helpers. Hue was away most of the time and was not aware of her responsibilities. Therefore, disagreements and discountenance were imminent when Hue inherited the responsibility of dealing with the domestic helpers. After dismissals, he had tried to maintain things single-handedly.

Courageously, he tried to prepare for the Pastor and his family; however, the task was challenging and was not successfully implemented. Recognition of what his wife, Jonnie Mae, had accomplished was now appreciated as never before. Everything was immaculate when she was alive. Hue was not prepared for her death. At this point, he felt a twinge of guilt as he recollected his unfaithfulness.

Hue's mind flashed back to some years ago when he visited St. Luke's Church where Jonnie Mae was the secretary. It was his desire to seduce her right away. Jonnie Mae's nonchalance and distant action made him want her all the more. Usually Hue had to do very little or nothing to gain the attention of a lady. However, this one was different in many ways, and the strait-laced lady made it clear that the only way he could bed her was to marry her.

Hue loved her, but he knew then that he could not be faithful to her, but he had to have her one way or the other.

Many of the ladies in the congregation had eyes on him ever since he joined the church, and they were devastated when they discovered that Hue and Jonnie Mae had married on a May weekend.

Jonnie Mae was a proud lady; however, she had skepticisms about her husband's unfaithfulness. No matter what she heard, she continued to live in denial, for she tried rationalizing Hue's faults away.

At this moment in his life, Hue felt that he was reaping just some of what he had sowed, as he looked out the window and noticed that Tom was delivering the prospective minister and his family.

As Tom came to a complete stop, he stated "Well, here we are. This will be your home for a short period of time."

Carl Levi took a glance at the stupendous house, and he was so stunned that he felt that he had become asphyxiated. "Is this where we will be living? This is gr-e-a-t!!" he finally muttered.

As Clara slid out of the car, she enunciated, "Why, this is what I would love to have."

Kate and Kirk could barely wait for the car to stop before they jumped out squealing like pigs, "We-e-e like this! We-e-e like this! Are we going to stay here Mom?"

"Yes, for a while. One day we hope to have a house just as great as this one," Clara spoke with distinction.

Soldierly, the Levi family marched into Dr. Dawson's house with their suitcases resembling artillery. Apprehensively, Tom observed them as he drove off.

After Hue escorted the family around, the two men retired to the parlor. While talking and drinking Corona Extra beer, Pastor Levi artfully learned everything about St. Luke's budget, and he was anxious to review it the first thing in the morning. He became cognizant of the monetary abundance. He also became aware that St. Luke had not had the responsibility of a salaried pastor for six years. In addition, during his inquisition he became knowledgeable that Joe Truss, as a broker and the treasurer of the Board of Directors, had invested the church money wisely. During these times, the stock market was escalating and Joe, as an advisor, had taken advantage of these opportunities.

Thereupon, Hue asked, "So, you would like to build a home here in Kingston?"

"Yes, I would like to start right away, so that we could get out of your house."

"How much would you like to put down on the home?" Hue asked.

Leaning back in the black leather chair, resembling the thinking man, Pastor Levi stammered, "O-O-Oh, we don't have any money just yet, but we should have about a half million in a few months. You see I was in a car accident, and the settlement should come through soon. Being a man of God, we donated all of our old furniture and clothes to charity. If the church could advance us some money to begin the construction, we would reimburse you with our blessings when we receive them."

Somewhat tipsy from the beer, Hue exclaimed, "Oh yes! You'll be able to get the advance. I am Doctor Hue Dawson, and what Hue wants, Hue gets."

Now, Pastor Levi wasn't feeling the beer at all, for his system had become immune to spirits over the years. He asked in excitement, "Will you put it in motion at our first board meeting?"

Feeling a little sluggish, Hue said in slow motion, "I-will-do-that-for-you, and I, I guarantee-e-e, you'll get – get it." Instantly, he fell over on the day bed and went to sleep.

Chapter III

The First Weeks

Enthusiasm was contagious in Kingston, for everyone was excited about the arrival of the new minister. People from the near-by towns inquired about joining in the celebration. Food connoisseurs began their preparations for the installation dinner.

On a cool fresh Sunday afternoon, the sun hid behind the fluffy white clouds while inside St. Luke Church, a new minister from Philadelphia was being installed. With prayers, praise and thanksgiving, happiness permeated the church.

Following the installation, a soulful dinner was served. Each table was decorated with celestial floral arrangements, and a delectable buffet dinner laden an elongated table with candelabrums lit at both ends. The delicious food consisted of fried and baked chicken, honey baked ham, barbeque ribs, smoked turkey, potato salad, spiced spaghetti, mashed potatoes with brown gravy, macaroni and cheese, baked beans, black-eyed peas, spinach salad, toss salad, string beans, collard greens, hard and soft rolls and cornbread.

The members were aware of the fact that it would not be a feast without desserts. Holly made their favorite sweet potato cakes, and many other cakes were donated. There were pies of many kinds, cobblers and puddings. Of course, Tom served homemade ice cream of many flavors, and Sue Ann served ice tea, punch and juice, but her lemonade made the splash. The joyful, thankful members and guests ate, drank, talked and laughed the evening away.

Afterward, when Tom and Sarah returned home, Sarah inquisitively stated, "Pastor Levi and Clara didn't seem very warm or appreciative, but maybe that was just my perception."

Trying to disguise his feeling about the matter, Tom stated, "You do have the capacity for great insight; however, we should give them time to adjust to a new environment."

With a sign of disgust, Sarah expounded on the introduction speech that Pastor Levi presented, "It seemed that he was not prepared to meet the congregation today."

Tom wanted to be optimistic, "Well, we will see what happens later. He is new to ministry, so maybe as time passes, he will improve." He then changed to a more cheerful topic.

During the following week, Hue and Pastor Levi continued to confer, and it was discovered that the Levi family was impecunious. The only things that they owned were in the flimsy suitcases that they transported from the train station. In spite of Pastor Levi's situation, he convinced Hue to take his suggestion before the Board of Directors.

With glorification, the Board of Directors and the new Pastor of St. Luke Church assembled for their first board meeting. Expressions of exultation were flowing from the members' lips as they greeted the Pastor Carl Levi. After all greetings and introductions were completed, Tom Best, the president of the Board of Directors, began, "The meeting will please come to order." Then he welcomed Pastor Levi and bestowed upon him a friendly message with best wishes from the Board of Directors at St. Luke Church. The meeting continued as he stated, "The secretary will read the minutes from the previous meeting." Secretary, Sammy, read the minutes. The president continued, "You have heard the minutes. Are there any corrections?" After a pause, he stated, "If not, they stand approved as read." Continuing, the president asked for the treasurer's report. Whereas, Pastor sat forward with attentiveness and scribbled in his pad as Joe Truss reported on the funds received and disbursed. In conclusion he reported the current balance in the treasury. Pastor's face revealed gratification when Joe disclosed the balance. Tom glanced at Pastor Levi, and then asked for committee reports. All the committee reports were presented, discussed and some ideas were tabled until the next meeting. Tom proceeded, "Thank you for your reports. Are there any other committee reports? If not, we shall proceed with the unfinished business. Is there any unfinished business?" At that point in time, some unfinished business was discussed. The transactions were executed in a calm, businesslike fashion. Solutions to the problems were efficiently accomplished.

The Board of Director's meeting moved on. Tom began the period of new business by saying, "Is there any new business to come before the Board of Directors?"

Hue raised his hand and stated, "Mr. Chairman."

Tom, the chairman responded, "Dr. Hue Dawson has the floor."

Dr. Dawson began, "I move that St. Luke Church appropriates $100,000.00 to Pastor Levi for him to begin the construction of a home."

Tom asked, "Is there a second?" There was no response. Tom repeated, "Is there a second?"

Seeing this matter inescapable, Sammy spoke up, "I second the motion."

Tom then said, "It has been moved and seconded that St. Luke Church appropriates $100,000.00 to Pastor Levi to begin the construction of a new home. Is there any discussion?"

Naturally, this was when the fracas began. Some of the board members attacked Hue like a group of hymenopterous insects. Hue's words of enticement were shaky; however, he was confident because he felt that he had done his homework with the majority of the board members.

After words went back and forth and to and fro, Pastor Levi thought he would make his final plea, for he was not sure of the **Dr.**'s influence on the board. Expeditiously, Pastor Levi told about his settlement, "I was in a car accident some time ago. A settlement should come through soon which should be a few months – it **will** be about a half million or more. I will repay as soon as this blessing comes through."

Politely, Joe waited for Pastor Carl Levi to finish his declaration of pursuit, then he said, "I think that we have spent enough time on this outrageous idea! We are not imbeciles!"

Tom was also ready to conclude the deliberation, so he pounded the gavel on the table. Silence permeated the room. At that particular point in time, he stated, "Are you ready for the question?" Tom paused and no one spoke, so he put the question to vote. "The question is on the motion to appropriate $100,000.00 to Pastor Levi to begin the construction of a home. Please indicate your pleasure by a show of hands. Those in favor?" Tom paused to count two hands. "Those opposed?" Tom paused again and observed the majority. "There were two in favor and ten opposed. The motion is denied."

Sweet Peppers-Sour Grapes & Wild Flowers

Tom, the chairman, did not vote; however, he had expressed his opinion early on, for he felt that it was a preposterous suggestion. Matter of fact, to him, it seemed to be downright ridiculous. In actuality, it should not have had the opportunity to be carried through a motion, but he was attempting to respect the incoming Pastor.

Thereupon, Tom asked, "Is there any more new business to come before the board?"

Hue was tenacious in his opinions, for he raised his hand once more, "Mr. Chairman."

Tom thought, "What will it be this time?" However, he knew he **must** recognize his hand. He reluctantly responded, "Dr. Hue Dawson."

Hue politely stated, "I move that St. Luke Board of Directors advances Pastor Levi $1,000.00 to tide him over until he receives his salary."

Whereupon, Tom asked, "Is there a second to this motion?"

This time, Sue Ann stated, "I second the motion."

With hopes that the board members would reveal some sympathy in this discussion, Tom stated, "It has been moved and seconded that St. Luke Board of Directors advances Pastor Levi $1,000.00 to tide him over until he receives his salary. Is there any discussion?"

Silence permeated the room, until Joe broke the silence, "If he is in need, as Christians, it appears to me that we could lend him a helping hand."

Kathy spoke up, "I will reiterate what Joe has just said. Pastor Levi **is** embarking upon a new career, so maybe he does need assistance."

Most of the board members were bobbing their heads up and down which indicated mutual understanding. They seemed to have been working together in harmony. Tom felt a twinge of euphoria, for everything was so peaceful.

Kathy then stated, "Mr. Chairman, I suggest that you call for the question."

Consequently, Tom asked, "Are you ready for the question?"

No one spoke after Tom gave a reasonable pause, so again he put the question to vote. "The question is in the motion to advance Pastor Levi $1,000.000 to tide him over until he receives his salary. Will you please voice your pleasure by a show of your hands? Those in favor?" There was a pause; wherein, all the board members raised their hands.

Continuing because of proper procedure, Tom stated, "Those opposed?" This time, no one raised his hand. "The motion passes," Tom then stated.

When there was no more new business, Tom took the opportunity to make several announcements. He reminded the group of the scheduled membership growth activities and the dates and time of the Sunday school drama club practice.

Sue Ann announced the upcoming Black History Events in and around the city.

Whereupon, Kathy stated, "Mr. Chairman, I move that the meeting be adjourned."

Hue ensued, "Second!"

Tom exhilaratingly announced, "Meeting is adjourned."

Instantly, Pastor Levi stood and strolled around the table as he gave each board member a weak handshake. With a cunning grin, he stated, "It was good negotiating with you. The future looks very promising."

Dr. Hue Dawson sat in disbelief, for he had experienced a terrible let down with his first motion. It was his belief that he had a great influence over most of the board members because of his standing in the community, and that first motion should have passed. "Anyway, he had accomplished something," he thought.

Some of the board members felt that Dr. Dawson took advantage of situations for his own selfish goods. Apparently, he wanted to be relieved of the bothersome Levi family, but for some unknown reason he was avoiding disclosing it.

Hue was in distress within his own home. For unknown reasons, he did not stand up to the wayward family. He became totally responsible for the food and living conditions of the family. The children were ravenous eaters and demanded their favorites from the spineless Hue. He was an excellent experienced cook, for he worked as a cook to finance his college and medical school.

Unbeknown reasons to the board members, Hue tried desperately to please the Levi family. Hue even put the dishes in the dishwasher after each dinner while Carl would retreat to the library, and Clara would retreat to the bedroom. Carl would announce that he had to prepare for Sunday's sermon and also work on his Master's in

Divinity dissertation, which he did all week. There was no effort to visit the sick at the hospital or make any calls to the shut-ins. The church office was inaccessible most of the week; therefore, no one was on call for emergencies. Sunday school, Bible school, Youth groups, Choir and Organizational meetings continued to be supervised by members of the church.

Frequently, Pastor Levi would fabricate excuses. One of his excuses was that he had a hearing problem because his hearing aids needed repairing. At this point, the congregation was not aware of the hearing problem; however, the members were very compassionate.

The last Sunday in February, the reluctant ushers and the skeptical members, sympathetically, made an extra collection for a new hearing aid. Of course, the collection was matched by an internal organization. Pastor Levi insinuated to the board members, "Maybe, I could purchase them from the same place that I got the old ones; I could do mail order." The members disagreed and insisted that Tom should arrange to go with him. The next week, Tom and Pastor Levi successfully purchased a new hearing aid.

Indeed, Clara had excuses also when she would retreat to the bedroom after dinner, for she had an excuse of being tired, and she felt that she needed more rest. Clara could sleep for fifteen successive hours a day, and she was growing like an inflated balloon. She didn't seem to have an ounce of energy. Nellie said that - *"the bed was sapping her energy."*

At the March Board meeting, Pastor Levi announced that he needed monetary assistance with his children's schooling. He proposed $100.00 monthly additional finance. Kate and Kirk had matriculated into private school.

It really bothered Tom to see how the Levi family was tenaciously trying to siphon the church's money; therefore, he immediately disagreed. "That should be your responsibility!"

"Remember, all of this money and more will be repaid in a few months!" the Pastor proclaimed in a calm pastoral tone.

"Are you sure?" Tom vocalized.

"Definitely!" he affirmed using his strongest voice.

Joe spoke up, "This is NOT our responsibility!"

The intensity of Hue's voice penetrated the room, "We don't mind assisting *our* Pastor with his children's education."

Feeling dominated by the others, Tom and Joe had an instinctive feeling that they were in the minority. To limit the debate, Tom called for a vote, "Those in favor of increasing the Pastor's salary $100.00 a month, please raise your right hand." Tom delivered a repugnant paused and continued. "Those opposed to increasing the Pastor's salary $100.00 a month, please raise your right hand.

Even with Tom, Sue Ann and Joe's disapproval, the majority sanctioned the proposal.

Tom made announcements, and then asked for germane announcements from the members.

Sue Ann announced the celebration of Black History Month in March because the celebration of the new minister predominated February.

"Mr. Chairman, I move that the meeting be adjourned," stated Joe Truss.

"I second the motion," replied Kathy.

"It has been moved and seconded that this Board of Directors' meeting is adjourned," Tom announced with a sigh of relief that it concluded on time, even though it was a troublesome meeting.

Chapter IV

Black History Month

    The St. Luke congregation prepared to commence their Black History Celebration on the next Sunday in March. Pastor Levi had very little knowledge of the meaning of Black History Month. As he perused the Sunday's program, he proclaimed, "These are **not** the kind of songs we should sing here at St. Luke's Church. Why is it necessary to completely transform our service for one month?"

    "This is our heritage. Wait and see, for you might gain some insight in our History," answered Holly who insisted that the program remain unchanged. She had become a little familiar with Pastor's hostility because she periodically assisted in the office. Reluctantly, he did not alter the program on the first Sunday.

    The congregation and choir sang - *Swing Low Sweet Chariot, Go Tell It on the Mountain, We Are Climbing Jacob's Ladder-* and many more. Erstwhile, the congregation sat motionless throughout the hour service; however, this particular Sunday these inspirational songs motivated some of them to bob their heads, sway or at least pat a foot. With tight-lips, Pastor Levi exhibited intimidation. Clara sat with folded arms, and her face presented contemptuousness. Kate and Kirk looked scared to death. The service was culminated with – *'Lift Every Voice and Sing'*. Whereby, the ninety voices resounded and transmitted an intonation of five hundred voices.

    When everyone stood, Pastor Levi vacillated for a while, but finally stood. Indecisiveness caused Clara to linger in her seat a little longer. Kate and Kirk stood after Sarah whispered to them. "You should always stand when the National Anthem is played or sung, so will you please stand?" Obstinately, Kirk stood, and Kate ensued. It seemed that the family had never been exposed to Blackness, even though Clara, Kate and Kirk were considered constituents of the Black race.

    As Sarah and Tom strolled out of church, Sarah whispered to Tom, "We'll eventually educate them about us." With a smile, Tom replied, "Yes, they got baptized in Blackness today."

Mary Flowers Carter

Sue Ann, Sarah, Tom and others diligently labored to accomplish a Black History Program that would be presented on the next Sunday afternoon. "This will be another learning experience for Pastor Levi and his family," Sue Ann chuckled.

Hue invited one of his associates and friend to be the main speaker. Graciously, Dr. John Simmons accepted the invitation. His travels were extensive, and he had collected a comparatively vast numbers of African artifacts. Sarah posted laminated pictures and photos of African Americans around the room. Red, black and green radiated the room with each table representing a renowned African American. Talent was superabundant at St. Luke and everyone contributed and donated.

Elegantly, Dr. John Simmons expounded on the topic: *'The Road We Have Traveled, But Where Do We Go From Here?'* When he enumerated the encounters on the road that Blacks had traveled, it was the congregation's desire that some of Pastor Levi's illusions would perish.

At the conclusion of the program, everyone stood to sing the National Anthem. Promptly, the Levi Family rose to their feet and stood erect as if they were in the military.

With tremendous dissatisfaction with the last two Sunday services and the unfathomable Sunday afternoon program, Pastor was determined to prepare the program for the third Sunday in March. He concocted a reason for Holly to be absent from the office, " You have been very faithful assisting in the office, and remember you are just a volunteer. Go home and take care of your family."

Holly apprehensively departed with an appreciative, "Thank You, Pastor Levi." She knew she had zillions of domestic things to do. Dropping items in the desk drawers and piling papers in the corners, she was out the door in a flash.

Immediately after Holly exited the door, Pastor Levi commenced to thinking about the ingredients that would be inscribed between the covers of this program. Deceit was written on his face. Zealously, he searched the Hymnal for songs that had been recently translated from German to English. Those were the ones that the congregation had never sung. Reluctantly, he exclusively included the National Anthem, *'Lift Every Voice and Sing'* on the inside back cover. Since he was not well-read or well-versed in Black literature, he was unaware of the forgery he was about to commit. He counterfeited the hymn by altering some words in the first verse – *'list'ning'* to *'listening'* and in the second verse – *'chast"ning'* to *'chastening'*. In verse one he inserted *'moral'* before the word *'victory'*. Making headway, he deleted *'unborn,'* and replaced the word *'fathers'* with *'parents'*. Convinced that he should exhibit his braininess, he changed *'drunk'* to *'drink'*.

Exhilarated by the thought that the members at St. Luke would now recognize him as the "all-powerful" LEADER, he was possessed by an exhilarating sensation. What he didn't know was that he had made a 'boo boo'. He had deprecated the hymn that was written by James Weldon Johnson, and he had also belittled the African American race.

Needless to say, this Sunday, St. Luke had an infuriated congregation. The church members felt that they were compelled to take action about this kind of behavior. On Sunday afternoon, telephones were busy. Tom, the president of the congregation, received numerous of calls. To each caller, he expressed his disappointment and promised that he would definitely meet with the Pastor as soon as the two could determine a mutual time and place.

Tom and Pastor Levi met at the Wright's Steak House the following Tuesday for a late lunch. At the inception of the conversation, Tom asked, "Why did you insist on printing such unfamiliar hymns in the bulletin for us to try to tackle?"

Having spent much time in Germany, he replied, "Those are the Germans' favorite hymns."

Still trying to exhibit respect for the Pastor, Tom exclaimed in an aggravated tone, "We are not in Germany; we are in America!"

Wiggling his nose and fluttering his eyelashes, Pastor proclaimed haughtily, "You all should try to broaden your horizon, and furthermore…"

Exasperation was seeping in as Tom interrupted Pastor, " Hell! JUST forget that for just now! We'll move on to the next topic that we **must** discuss – for the members of St. Luke are outraged about your altering some of the words in **OUR** National Anthem."

"Well, let's see here. Do yo-ou happen to have a bulletin with you?" inquired Pastor with a sound of intimidation.

Without hesitation, Tom reached in his pocket and ostentatiously presented the bulletin.

Tom's body language was so defiant that Pastor decided to explain each and every metamorphosis. "I was under the assumption that 'list'ning' and 'chast'ning' were misspelled. When I inserted 'moral', it supported my text for my sermon. As you can remember, I revealed a research study that stated that the largest percentage of churchgoers was African Americans, and on the other hand, the largest percentage of immoral citizens was African Americans. I also apprised YOU-ALL of the multitude of crimes committed in cities by African Americans. Also, take a look at the number of unwed mothers in St. Luke Church."

With perseverance, Tom continued chewing on his steak, " Now where did you do your doggone research?"

"At the Seminary," Pastor answered timidly.

"So *that* is what you were taught at a Seminary?" expounded Tom. "Go on – tell me more. I need to hear this."

Breathing a little easier, Pastor continued, "I felt that the word 'unborn' was an unnecessary word. Instead of 'fathers', we should have 'parents" in our homes, and 'drunk' refers to drunkenness which should not be sung in our church."

Exhibiting authority, Tom asked, "Do you know that you have committed a crime?"

Still trying to declare his brilliancy, Pastor explained, "Christians should be committed to growing in the grace and knowledge of their Savior and Lord."

Tom shook his head and stated very firmly, "From that statement, I can see that you are immature in the ministry, so I will consider this as a puerile deed. Matter of fact, I am going to **tr-y** to save your darn hide, for it may be impossible. **Ple-a-se** think or ask questions before you act from now on."

As Tom proceeded to move away from the table, he decided to give Pastor Levi a smidgen of hope. " I assume that you are still in the learning stage. I will try to prevent the Board of Directors from acting on this, and hopefully for your sake, it will not go before the voter's assembly. Good Day, Pastor! I must return to work."

Tom was an Attorney and Counselor at Law, for he possessed a facile mind that marked him as a shrewd lawyer. He was well known throughout the state of Virginia.

Back at Tom's residence, Sarah was returning home from school. She carried books and a briefcase overflowing with students' papers waiting to be checked and graded. As she opened the door, she could hear the telephone ringing. Struggling to get to the phone, she dropped her briefcase. Papers scattered around the room. Rushing toward the phone and picking it up on the third ring, she wheezed, "Hello!"

"Hello, Sarah! This is Sue Ann. You sound out of breath."

Still panting somewhat, Sarah whispered, "I was loaded with schoolwork, and I found it difficult to hurry in when I heard the telephone. Other than that, I'm fine."

"Good! Anyway, I called to remind you that Kate and Kirk's birthdays are on Friday. I think it would be only fitting if the Sunday School would give them a birthday party on Saturday when the children are out of school. Even if we are observing Black History Month, I think we should remember their birthday."

In full agreement, Sarah replied, "I think that's a wonderful idea. Is there anything I can do to help?"

"Yes! Thanks! By the way, you can. Today is Tuesday, and we would like to have the invitations in the children's hands tomorrow. If you would assist us, we will take the invitations to the children's houses. With the help of some of the Sunday School teachers, they will be ready by tomorrow morning."

Graciously accepting the assignment, Sarah responded, "I will be glad to assist in delivering birthday invitations. Just let me know who and where."

Delighted about the upcoming event, Sue Ann's voice carried a happy tone, "I am sure the Sunday School staff will take care of everything else. The children will be **ecstatic** when they discover that they are having a party. Please come by if you have the time. It will be from three to five in the afternoon. We plan to use room three in the Parish."

Sarah reflected for a moment, then she responded, "I'll probably drop some birthday gifts off, but I won't be able to stay because I have another engagement at that time on Saturday. Anyway drop those invitations off tomorrow morning, and I'll deliver them on my way to school tomorrow."

"Thank you, Sarah! See you tomorrow morning!"

Bright and early Wednesday morning, Sue Ann rang Sarah's doorbell. Sarah opened the door with a cheery, "Good Morning, Sue Ann! You and your helpers must have worked late last night."

With a broad smile, Sue Ann replied, "Good morning to you, Sarah! We really appreciate your help. We did work late, but we didn't mind. Thanks for your help."

Sue Ann said good-bye, and Sarah prepared for her distribution before school.

Overjoyed to have a party, the children started arriving early on Saturday afternoon. Sue Ann, Holly and the rest of the Sunday school staff were on hand to welcome them. The party somewhat held the atmosphere of an amusement park. Merriment permeated the decorative room. Colored helium balloons stood in every corner of the room and also served as centerpieces for the tables.

Pastor Levi, Clara and the twins were the last ones to arrive. Hand in hand Pastor and Clara strolled over to a corner. There they sat and whispered to each other like two lovebirds. Without hesitation, Kirk joined in the games. Kate gradually warmed up when she saw that the children were having lots of fun without her participation. When it was time for the children to break away from the games to eat, they did not hesitate. Holly had them to lineup to wash their hands. Then each child proceeded to the food line where there were pizzas, hotdogs, potato chips, popcorn, homemade cookies and pops of different flavors. Also, in keeping with a birthday party, there was a beautiful, delectable birthday cake that Kathy had baked and decorated. Kathy was a culinary student at the University. Kate and Kirk blew out their candles and made their wishes. The cake was then served with homemade ice cream that Tom had donated.

At the conclusion of the festivities, the children sat in a circular position while Kate and Kirk sat in the center. They proceeded to open their gifts while the children "oohed" and "aahed" over the

Sweet Peppers-Sour Grapes & Wild Flowers

beautiful gifts. With enthusiasm, they stripped away the lovely wrappings. From within the coverings, they removed dresses, pants, short sets, shirts, swimsuits, skates, electronic games, books, and many other educational materials. Happiness glowed on their faces.

When it was time to go, Clara did not offer to help cleanup. She and Pastor said, "Good evening", but not an appreciative word was uttered. They didn't even remind the children to say, "Thanks". Holly and Sue Ann knew that they would solve that problem in Sunday School on Sunday.

On the last Sunday in March was the finale of the Black History Celebration. During the service the congregation and choir sang Good Ole Negro Spirituals, stood boldly at the conclusion of the service and resounded, *"Lift Every Voice and Sing,"* and the echo was heard outside of the church.

Even on Sunday, Pastor did not mention the birthday party that the Sunday School staff had given the twins. When the twins were in Sunday School classes, Sue Ann asked Kate and Kirk to stand and thank the children for coming to the birthday party and for such lovely gifts. Kirk was the first one to stand, and he said, "Thank you for giving me a good birthday party. I like the gifts. And-and I had a good time. That's all."

The children said in unison, "You are welcome!"

Kate just sat and said, "Thanks," as she hunched her shoulders. Sue Ann insisted that she stand. She reluctantly stood while leaning on a chair. Holly carefully moved the chair with one hand while supporting Kate with the other. Everyone waited for Kate to speak. After waiting for a few seconds, she said, "Thanks."

Sue Ann asked, "Did you like the gifts? Did you enjoy the food and games?"

Kate murmured, "Yes."

"Yes. What?" Asked Holly.

A student became restless and unexpectedly she yelled out, "We enjoyed the party, and we loved **them** gifts!"

Right then and there, Kate said in a hurry, "I- enjoyed- the- party. I- love the- gifts."

All the students applauded and said, "You are welcome, Kate!"

A few days later, Pastor Levi mentioned to Tom that his children were harassed in Sunday School. Tom was aware of the incident because Holly and Sue Ann had spoken to him about it. Being prepared for the complaint from Pastor, Tom frankly stated, "Sometimes, we are in a position where we have to expand our Sunday School lessons if we see fit."

Pastor was unresponsive to the statement. He had a faraway look, as they discussed other matters.

Chapter V

The Advent Season

Advent Season had emerged upon parishioners in Kingston. The red breasted robins seemed to have been singing, "Oh, Come, Oh, Come, Emmanuel," for the parishioners at St. Luke. The members appreciated the robins' contribution to the season because it appeared that Pastor Levi had no intentions of including that particular song or any other song that depicted the Advent Season. He tenaciously continued to exercise restraint over the Sunday bulletins.

Adversity materialized on Palm Sunday at St. Luke. On that particular Sunday, members were accustomed to being detained in the vestibule of the church until the Pastor announced their entrance. Each member was provided with a palm branch as each one entered the vestibule. As they stood waiting for Pastor to lead the procession, Pastor Levi sat in the pulpit without a glance at the rear. Eventually, Sue Ann assumed the responsibility of going to ask Pastor to come to the vestibule and lead them into church.

As Sue Ann approached him and observed his expression, she could feel the adversity. With apprehension, she requested, "Pastor Levi, will you assume your responsibility and come and lead the members into church. This is Palm Sunday."

"That is not a part of our service today. Who took that responsibility to buy palm branches?" Pastor Levi snorted.

In astonishment, Sue Ann's eyes became as big as saucers as she stood looking steadily and intently.

Authoritatively, Pastor Levi demanded, "Show them the way inside the church!"

Overcome with stupefaction, Sue Ann's feet seemed to have been glued to the floor. Her legs seemed to have weighed a ton, and her body seemed to have become inanimate.

"Did you hear what I said? Ask them to come in and be seated!" Pastor Levi reiterated in a louder voice.

With determination, Sue Ann elucidated the reason for her request as she whispered with a soft hushed sound, *"Pastor Levi, we are* accustomed to marching into church on Palm Sunday and waving our palm branches. The reason for this is that on this day, the Blessed Lord Jesus entered Jerusalem, riding on a donkey..."

Pastor Levi held his hand up in a stop position as he interrupted her before she could finish, "In case you are not aware of it, I **am** the minister, and I **have** studied the bible, and I am quite scholarly in theology. This is St. Luke and not Jerusalem. Things **will** be changing around here!" Majestically, he rose from his seat, stepped forward and stood erect in front of the church while he beaconed for the members to come forward.

Reluctantly, the choir members led the procession while they sang the unfamiliar song from the program that he had prepared. The song had no denotation of Easter.

Sue Ann made a definite attempt to forget the incident. Gracefully, she rejoined in with the parishioners and strolled proudly to her seat while waving her palm branch back and forth.

Pastor Levi's sermon had begun to have a flavor of admonishment. Primarily, on this Palm Sunday he spoke of, 'Vengeance upon those that did not love the Lord and a church of unbelievers'. After the service, the parishioners departed in a somber mood. However, Sue Ann caught up with Pastor before he departed. Trailing behind him, she called, "Pastor Levi!"

Pivoting on his heels, he made a sudden stop, and there was almost a head on collision. With an astonishing look, he uttered, "Yes!" He seemed to have been anticipating an attack.

Making an effort to relax him, Sue Ann stated, "No problems! Just have a question to ask you."

"What's that?" he asked as if he were in a hurry.

Sue Ann made an honest endeavor to be very tactful, "Does Clara need any help in preparing the thank you notes for the twins' birthday party?"

"I'm sure she will take care of that. Is that all?" Pastor asked as if he were anticipating something else.

Sue Ann gave the matter careful thought, then she said, "It seems to be taking quite a while, so I thought she might need some help."

"Nope!" was all he said as he walked off.

When Sue Ann returned home, she reported to Sarah the outcome of her conversation with Pastor Levi. Sue Ann suggested that Sarah go and visit Clara, but Sarah was not too sure of such a brazen move.

Sweet Peppers-Sour Grapes & Wild Flowers

On Good Friday, Sarah was on Spring break from Kingston School. She loved her kindergarten children, but it was refreshing to have a break from them. She felt a sense of relief on this beautiful bright sunny morning. Stretching as she rose from her incredible night of sleep, she crept downstairs and found her usual breakfast prepared for her. As she came through the doorway, Tom peered up from the newspaper, "Good morning, sweetheart!"

"Good morning, Honey," Sarah replied cheerfully. "Did you have a good night's sleep? You are up so early."

As Tom rubbed his hand across his forehead, he responded, "Um, pretty good, I guess. It seems that there is a lot to think about these days and nights."

Sarah felt that this was an opportune time to discuss Clara. As she observed Tom, he seemed to be receptive, so she began, "From my observation, Clara is not adjusting to her new church environment. She persistently sits in the back of the church, and she is very undemonstrative. Consequently, I have gone out of my way to make her feel welcome. However, Clara was not reciprocal. Also, she has made no attempt to respond to the people who gave gifts to the family and assisted them in other ways."

To Sarah's surprise, Tom voiced, "Maybe, you should visit her."

"Just, maybe, that's a good idea! Sue Ann made the same suggestion," she replied as she rose from the table. With a continuation of cheerfulness, she took two steps at a time as she dashed upstairs to prepare for her visit. Humming a song as she swiftly slipped into the shower and was out in a jiffy. Consuming lesser time for primping, she was dressed in a few seconds and was ready to go. Dramatically, she slipped on her bright red sweater, and without any more deliberation with Tom, she kissed him on the cheek and was on her way to visit Clara.

As Sarah approached the house, she realized that visiting Clara was an impetuous move. Gradually ascending the steps, she gazed around; she noticed that the beautiful flowers in the garden appeared horrendous, and the grass that was once emerald green was now a dreadful brown. As she stepped on the porch, she noticed that the screen door was torn and the windows were dirty. She thought, *"Why, Jonnie Mae must be turning over in her grave."*

Sarah rang the doorbell; the children hollered and screamed as both of them raced to open the door. They began fighting at the door.

Kirk screamed, "I can get it!" It seemed as if Kate and Kirk were pushing and hitting each other.

Then Kate hollered, "Leave me alone, I know how to open the door!"

"You never can open it because you don't know how!" came the other voice.

"Well, I can learn!"

"Move! I said move!" "Bop, bop, slap," came the sounds.

"Oh, you bit me!"

"Well, you scratched me!"

At this point, Sarah was ready to walk away from the door when she heard Clara call, "Who is it children?"

Sarah heard them holler, "Why, it's Ms. Best!"

Sarah came back and stood patiently by the door while the lethargic Clara slowly opened it. Kirk and Kate were standing wide-eyed to one side as if they were sizing Sarah up. As Clara looked in the mirror near the door, she said, "Hi there, Sarah. Will you please come in? How long have you been out here?"

After taking a deep breath and a sigh, Sarah said, "Well it seemed like hours, but I hope you're ok."

"Well, really, I'm not ok."

"What is the problem?" Now as Sarah finished the sentence, she realized that she never should have asked.

Clara began, "I have had a headache for two days because I have a tooth that needs repairing. I need some dental work. The insurance plan should be in effect in a few days, and then I will begin my dental work."

Sarah was thinking, *"She needs dental work. So, she didn't have dental insurance until our church put it into effect. With all these problems, how can I mention thank you notes?"*

Clara continued, "I didn't sleep last night because I had stomach cramps that was caused by the Ibuprofen that I took for the toothache."

All Sarah could think to say was, "It seems that one problem led to another."

Clara went on, "Not only that, Hue cooked those darn pinto beans that gave me gas, and I thought I was having a heart attack, for I started to wake Carl and ask him to take me to emergency."

"Too bad! Well anyway, how are things coming along as far as finding your house?" Sarah interjected.

"We haven't found anything that we desire that's affordable. It seems to be taking so long, for I thought we would be in our own home by now."

Sarah thought, "You should be ashamed to reside in someone's home for this period of time." Just then Clara yawned and stretched, Sarah could see that she had grown even larger since she had come to Kingston. Nellie had quietly mentioned to Sarah that Clara wanted to go shopping for new clothes for Easter. She could see why now, for she had surely outgrown the few clothes that she had brought with her.

At this point in time, Sarah was sick of this pessimistic person and wanted to end it all by saying, "Good bye and Good riddance," but she was curious about the upkeep of the inside of this yesteryear mansion. She took a stroll over in front of the fireplace where she could definitely see in other rooms. As far as she could see, the place looked more like a pig's sty. Children's clothes were all over the floor; the kitchen sink was full of dirty dishes, and shoes were everywhere. It was no wonder that Dr. Dawson had begun to spend night and day at the office. His beautiful home had been maliciously taken over.

Now that Pastor Levi was receiving a salary and had procured a $100.00 increase the second month on the alleged job, he was able to buy groceries for the family. Hue had mentioned that they could barely make it from paycheck to paycheck because when it came to money, they seemed to have a hidden agenda. Hue also disclosed that he had discontinued the cooking, and, of course, Clara didn't cook, and fast food was a regular.

As Sarah continued to survey the locale, Clara seemed to possess a desire to chitchat. Consequently, she proceeded to elaborate on her husband's background, and she relayed detailed information. Carl Levi had been married before which was presented in his resume. He married his high school sweetheart, Laura, who was a stripper in a nightclub. Trying to guard her and protect her from insults, he sat night after night devouring drinks at the bar while waiting for her to conclude her performances. After a few months into their marriage,

Laura became pregnant. Conscientiously, she fulfilled her duties at the club until her baby, Millie, was born. After the birth of Millie, she remained at home because of Carl's insistence; however, she was miserable. Despondence was a realization when she began to neglect little Millie, Carl and the house. The tension in the home induced many altercations. Trying to understand Laura's propensity to dance, he reluctantly permitted her to return to work.

Possessed with enthusiasm about her job, Laura disavowed the responsibility of motherhood and wife. Returning home late was an occurrence that was becoming more frequent. Customarily, Millie would reside at the dwellings of friends, neighbors or just plain acquaintances. Many nights, Laura did not bother to inquire about her whereabouts, and Millie would remain at the residence for several days.

Carl Levi, who was working as a car salesman, was inebriated incessantly. His down-in-the-dumps spirit was exhibited by his slovenly dress code. He was becoming ineffective and unproductive, and his careless mistakes were costing the company a monetary loss.

On the day that he was dismissed from his job, he was stricken with a heart attack. Things were touch-and-go for a few days. The uncertainty of Carl's stability impelled the hospital officials to summon Laura to his bedside. She spotted the chaplain on her way in, and persuaded him to join her for her visit.

Laura collaborated with the chaplain, Pastor Carson. As she explained her intentions to release herself from all marriage obligations, she begged him to look after Carl.

Being dependable, Pastor Carson obliged Laura, for he was a believer in the faith of healing. Whereby, his convictions seemed to have had an effect on Carl. During his recuperation period, Pastor visited him as frequently as time would allow. As the days elapsed, it was quite apparent that his body and soul were healing. Carl realized the blessings of being endowed with a devoted friend and excellent insurance coverage.

Eventually, Carl was released from the hospital with the stipulations that he would follow doctor's orders. His assurance of support would be a daily visiting nurse. After returning home from his heart surgery, he began recuperating slowly with the assistance of her -Nurse Clara Mae Hill. When he first laid eyes on her, her shapely body enraptured him. Every morning, he was filled with anticipation, and before long, he burst forth and kissed her "Good Day".

Laura filed for a divorce and had flown the coop with some strange guy that she had met at the nightclub where she worked. Carl did not contest the divorce. A couple, that had conscientiously taken care of Millie and regarded her as their very own, was adopting her.

Pastor Carson was a regular visitor and soon convinced Carl that he should become a theologian. Presently, a promising future seemed unconceivable because he had just about sopped up all his savings and investments during his convalescence.

Clara continued and her eyes became misty. She shared how she disclosed every inch of her life to Carl. She revealed that she had been jilted by her boyfriend just weeks before the wedding; therefore, she was very vulnerable. Indeed, they both found that the regurgitation was very therapeutic. In a sneaky way, Carl became knowledgeable about all of her finances. His heart infirmity had caused him to become penniless overnight.

The two consentaneously had a sexual affair. Everything was electrifying and breathtaking until she heard Carl announce, "The fornication was sensational!" Obviously, she thought of it as 'lovemaking'. Trying to rectify the statement, he exclaimed, "At least it wasn't adultery because we are both unmarried." Moreover, she was thin-skinned and perceived the shrewd remarks as rejection. Hence, she was dumb-founded when Carl suddenly asked her to marry him. She decided not to perpetuate the situation and gave him an affirmative 'yes'.

Thus, they were married, and afterward, he matriculated into a Midwestern Bible College. During this time, Kate and Kirk were born. Thereafter, he studied in Germany. He had reestablished residence in the states when he received his call to St. Luke. Promptly, he accepted the call.

Sarah was overwhelmed with the news and felt this was confidential; therefore, she **would** be closemouthed about the Levis' personal affairs. As she observed Clara's somber expression, she felt very uncomfortable. She began searching her mind for departure remarks. "Well, that was quite a story -- I think I'll be on my way -- hope you feel better," Sarah, apprehensively, stated as she ambled out the door and into the fresh air. The outside had never felt so invigorating, nor had it ever looked so wholesome to her.

Taking a short cut down the winding pathway and through the apple orchard where she had taken her kindergarten class many times, Sarah could hardly wait to talk to Nellie, but she was not going to repeat the news story. As she walked along, she felt like Little Red Riding Hood who was off to visit her grandmother. She skipped and sang while the apple trees seemed to have been smiling at her. Ever so quietly, out from burrows and nests and hollow trees, crept the little woodland animals. Birds sang their gayest melodies, and all seemed to be filled with joy except Clara.

"Ring, ring," went Nellie's doorbell. Nellie had been out of the bed for hours working in the yard and garden. "Good morning, Nellie. Are you ready to receive a little company?" Sarah chirped.

With her captivating voice, Nellie stated, "Sure, anytime and good morning to you, and please tell me, where are you on your way to this beautiful Friday morning?"

"Tom made a suggestion this morning, and I impulsively considered. I'll tell you all about it when I get my breath," Sarah murmured.

Sarah entered Nellie's house, and it was so refreshing to see someone smiling and to be with someone who wasn't complaining or walking down memory lane. She gracefully sat on the divan and gave a sigh, "Huh!". She began, "I just left Clara's house or should I say Dr. Dawson's house, and what a junkie mess that house has become since the Levis have arrived."

"Yes, I really feel sorry for Hue. Because of the burdensome Levi family, he decided to reside at his office and the hospital until their house is completed," Nellie interjected.

Abruptly, Sarah inquired, "Nellie, did you tell me that Clara wants you to go shopping with her?"

As Nellie ingratiated Sarah with a cup of herbal tea, she stated, "Yes, we plan to go tomorrow. It seems that she wants to do some Easter shopping. I did not schedule piano classes for tomorrow, which will be 'Holy Saturday' anyway."

As Sarah sipped her tea, she continued, "It seems that she might be outgrowing what she has, and she spends a great deal of time in bed as if she is ill, for she said that she needs dental work done."

"Is it true that there is something wrong with her back also?" Nellie stated in a questionable tone.

That statement induced Sarah to reveal that Pastor Levi was very anxious about every detail of their insurance coverage because of Clara's intentions to undergo back surgery.

Sympathetically, Nellie replied, "It seems that she has a great deal of heath problems."

Suddenly, Sarah felt a twinge of compassion for the Levi family. She sprang to her feet and rolled her shoulder in one direction and then in the other, while she tried to get her mind off the Levi family.

Promenading down the path on her way to her residence, Sarah was saturated with contentment, for she had not mentioned any of the confidential stories that Clara had so willingly revealed. She was so proud of her uncompromisingness.

It was Holy Saturday; the April rain was falling, and the weather was fit for ducks as Clara climbed into Nellie's burgundy Mercedes. They were on their way to the mall for a shopping spree. Nellie was astounded at Clara's loquaciousness, for she reiterated all that she had related to Sarah and promised to continue after her shopping spree.

Once at the mall, Clara announced that she only shopped at such stores as Dillard's, Nordstrom's and Lord & Taylor's. The shopping spree began with Dillard's. There she scrutinized and inspected articles as she went in and out of the dressing room. It seemed that she was not satisfied with the mixing and matching at Dillard's, so she suggested that they proceed to Nordstrom's. Again, she undertook her characteristic shopping procedures. After about an hour or so, she desired to move ahead to Lord & Taylor's. Once at Lord & Taylor's, she continued to try on the finest and the most expensive of items. Now that she was about to make a decision, she complained to the saleslady when she could not find her favorite colors. Clara would stroll out of the fitting room with most of her dresses too tight, and as she glided around with her finger beside her nose, she would ask Nellie, "How does this look?"

Nellie was getting tired and exhausted, so she frankly stated, " I think it would look splendid if you would may-be –uh -get a size a little bit larger."

"But I am going to lose weight, and this will be just right in no time," Clara said as she twirled around and around on her heels.

"Well, don't you want to look okay now?" asked Nellie.

"You don't think I look okay in this?" Clara inquired exasperatedly.

"Buy it if you like," Nellie said in a cranky voice, for her shoes had begun to pinch her feet.

After trying on multitude of dresses and numerous of shoes in the department stores, Clara chose five of the most expensive Jones of New York, Anne Klein and Liz Claiborne dresses and five pair of the most expensive shoes with Coach, Dooney and Bourke bags to match. She handed the items to the saleslady and announced to her that Nellie would pay for them. Nellie was flabbergasted and with hesitation she tried to think of something, but it seemed that her little head, with its short trimmed Afro, had shrunk, and there was no room left for any more thoughts. During her bewilderment, the clerk anxiously waited while she fumbled in her purse and extradited her charge card with trembling fingers. She was also apprehensive about the fact that the total might take her over her credit limit. However, it seemed that she was at a point of no return. When the saleslady returned her card, smiled and said, "Thank you, Mrs. Gray. Have a good day," she was unresponsive. She retrieved the card and strolled out of the store.

Nellie silently drove home, while Clara continued to recapitulate her experiences. Her revelation began with their stay in Germany. She related the incident of her returning from a shopping trip. When she opened her front door, a young girl without a stitch on, ran out the door and down the steps and disappeared into the darkness. Bewildered and perplexed, Clara said that she staggered in and stumbled over to the divan, for she felt that her legs were made of rubber. During her discombobulation, Carl came down the stairs with a nonchalant expression on his face. He questioned her about her strange behavior. Clara said that she asked him about the girl that she had seen. Carl maintained that he was alone despite her persistence.

During the discussion the next few days, Carl made her believe that she had experienced disembodiment.

Nellie heard all of Clara's divulgence; however, her mind was on her money. Nellie thought, "Maybe I should have told her that I didn't have the money," but she remembered that Clara asked her on the way to the store if she had a charge card. She had told her that she had a charge at those particular department stores. As she dropped Clara off at her home, away–from-home, not only were her shoes pinching, but also her back was aching, and her head was throbbing. When she arrived home, she suddenly remembered that Clara had not even said a simple, *"Thank you, nor had she mentioned repayment plans."* She was sure that Clara had used her for a confidante today, so that she could swindle her money.

The day after the shopping spree was Easter Sunday, and it was a bright sunny warm morning. Pastor Levi appeared at church dressed in shorts, short sleeve shirt and sandals. The dignified sophisticated swarthy congregation was awe-stricken. With a sigh of relief, Sarah uttered to Tom, "It is a blessing that he will be wearing a robe in the pulpit."

Trying to suppress his astonishment, Tom bobbed his head as he muttered, "Uh-huh!"

Clara made sure that she was late for Church, so that she could stroll down the aisle in her new Easter clothes, for she felt that she was "Drop Dead" gorgeous in her matching elegant Ann Klein outfit. All the church members' eyes were definitely transfixed on her. There were whispers such as, "Where did she get those clothes?" "She thinks she is looking good." "Where does she think she is going – to a fashion show?"

The benumbed Nellie sat plunking away at the piano while she was feeling more like a "nincompoop" than a pianist. She was well aware of the fact that she had used poor judgment, for she had not even bought any new clothes for herself. The shoes that she was wearing were about six years old, and Lord knows she could not remember the year that she had purchased her pink suit.

Sunday after Sunday, since the arrival of Pastor Levi, Nellie had sat plunking away on the piano while everyone, including Pastor Levi, sat stone faced without singing. The selection of hymns was very unfamiliar to the congregation and the choir. Therefore, Nellie got a great deal of instrumental practice while the members mumbled whenever they could manage a tune.

About a couple of weeks earlier, Nellie called Pastor Levi on the phone, and to her surprise, he was in the church office. "Good afternoon, St. Luke Church. This is Pastor Levi speaking."

"Good afternoon, this is Nellie Gray. Pastor Levi, I have something that I would like to discuss with you. Do you have a few minutes to spend with me this afternoon?"

"Yes, I'll be here at the office for the next hour. I'll have to pick Kate and Kirk up from school because Clara isn't feeling well."

"Well, I'll be there in a few minutes."

Filled with optimism, Nellie rushed out the door, ran to the garage, jumped into her Mercedes and speedily drove to the church office.

As she entered the church office, he rose behind his desk and said, "Have a seat please."

She gracefully sat down as she began to express her thoughts, "Pastor Levi, I am very concerned about our selection of hymns for Sunday morning services, for the congregation seems to be unfamiliar with the …."

Before she could finish, he asserted, " You all probably want to sing some of those spirituals that are not appropriate for our services."

Nellie was trying to keep her composure. She sat up straight, but instantaneously, her neck moved around as if it were made of rubber as she pointed her finger and came out with, "You…you...."

Before she could finish, Pastor Levi quickly said, "Oh, I don't mean any harm, but you know this is an Evangelical church."

Nellie exclaimed, "Maybe I should go before I say something that would cause me to lose my religion!" She stood, strolled over to the desk and articulated, "I made a list of familiar songs from our hymnal, and here they are. Please take a look at them, and we would like for you to consider some of them." She placed the list on his desk as she released a casual, "good evening," and departed the premises.

Sweet Peppers-Sour Grapes & Wild Flowers

That was about three weeks ago, and to this day, not a single song on the list had been chosen. Thoroughly disgusted with her powerlessness as a musician and her inability to handle the shopping situation with Clara, her mind became jumbled and her music suddenly got off key.

Holly, who was standing nearest the piano, whispered, "Are you ok, Nellie?"

Nellie bobbed her head up and down which meant- "Yes." She then made a more concerted effort to finish the music for the service.

Chapter VI

More Frustrations

Hue had spent a couple of days at the hospital, and he was exhausted. As he drove home, the April rain poured down. The storm clouds blotted out the stars across the inky blackness, yellow lightning flashed, and thunder rumbled angrily. Driving into his driveway, the beams of his headlight reflected bikes and skates in his driveway. Hue was praying constantly to be patient with the Levi's slovenliness, but somehow an uncontrollable feeling of frustration consumed him as he opened his car door and lunged from the car – flinging bikes and skates to the side. He gnashed his teeth with anger as he climbed in the car and drove into the garage.

Since the rain had stopped, the clouds had parted and the friendly moon was shining through, he decided to take a walk around and take in some fresh air. Right before his very eyes, Hue could see the deterioration of his yard and garden. Trying to think of a remedy to the situation, his mind reflected on Sammy Jones. Sammy did maintenance for the church; meantime, he probably could give him a few hours at his house. Without hesitation, Hue rapidly went into the house and called Sammy.

A lady answered the phone. "Hello." He recognized Sue Ann's voice. "Sue Ann, how are you? This is Hue Dawson."

"Fine, thank you for asking."

"May I speak to Sammy?"

"Yeah, you may." Hue could hear Sue Ann screaming, "Sam-m-y, Sam-m-y, pick up the telephone."

Sammy picked up the phone, "Hel-lo-o."

Hue began, "Sammy, I was wandering if you had some time to do some yard and garden work for me?"

"Let – me- see," Sammy answered as he scratched his head. Lord knows he really needed more money. "Could probably do it on Tuesday morning."

"Thank you. Thank you." Hue replied, "Just go right over and begin work even if I am not at home."

"Ok, Dr. Dawson, be glad to." Sammy placed the phone back on the hook, and with contemplation he stated, "Have some additional work to do. Dr. Dawson wants me to maintain his estate."

Bursting with exuberance, Sue Ann smiled while she pondered the good news. "When does he want you to begin?"

"Tuesday," Sammy replied hesitantly. He was aware of the reason Sue Ann was so excited. She yearned for the day that Sammy would ask her to marry him. He had repeated over and over, "When I am able, I will ask your hand in marriage."

"Just maybe, maybe, the time will come soon," thought Sue Ann. She was spending more time at Sammy's house than her own since her older sister, Tammy Lee, had returned from New York City. It seemed to her that Tammy was cantankerous most of the time, and they could not see *eye-to-eye,* so she started staying at Sammy's house, for this was a good excuse –not that she needed an excuse.

Sue Ann had never married, for she had no desire to marry until she met Sammy. In her childhood, she had "climbed many mountains and swum many oceans." She lived with her mother in the desolate country. Every time her mother turned her back, a cunning uncle or a devious cousin was lurking in the bushes licking his chops, peeping and peering at her with seductive intentions. In spite of the fact that she kept her watchful eyes opened, molestation did occur.

Once in a while, her mother had to take business trips. She would always kiss her and try to give her assurance by saying, "Hon, I will be gone for a day or two. If problems arise, your Uncle Will is right down the road, and your cousins over at the farmhouse will be at your beck and call." Little did her mother know, that these relatives were extremely contemptible creatures.

When she was about ten years old, her mother was barely out of sight when Uncle Will swaggered up the pathway and gently turned the doorknob, in that the door was never locked. When the door opened, Uncle Will swayed in with sleazy clothes and a devilish, saber-tooth grin. As he moved toward her with his glassy red inebriated eyes, she could smell the whiskey on his breath. He drunkenly whispered, "You sure have a big beautiful butt, and I must have it." Horrified, Sue Ann backed away until her trembling back was against the wall. He grabbed her viciously, and like a mad man, he ripped her clothes off and raped her. After that day, it seemed that there was always an altercation with an uncle or cousin, and she seemed to have been the loser. After the repetitive physical attacks, Sue Ann felt that her body was a living sacrifice to a demon.

"Those days are over," she said aloud to herself. At this particular point in time, she had Sammy, and this was a blissful era in her life. Currently, she was a dynamic member of the Board of Directors and a competent Sunday School teacher at St. Luke Church. Moreover, she was gainfully employed at Virginia State Bank.

Tammy's lifestyle was somewhat loose end while she was in New York. Now that she had returned to Kingston, she had rejoined St. Luke and had become a vital member of the choir. Her enchanting voice enhanced the sound of the music at the church. The members were pleasantly pleased to have her back.

On Tuesday morning, Sammy started cleaning the yard. As he cleaned under the library window, he noticed many miniature whiskey bottles beneath the window on the ground. Sammy's bony fingers grasped each bottle as his large round eyes glared at each one. His mind grew wearied as he counted …29, 30, 31, 32.. He put them in a paper bag that he found in his truck and vigorously continued his assignment. Desiring to finish in a hurry, he took long strides as he mowed the lawn, and when he shaped the shrubbery, he did it in an animated automatic fashion.

He was perspiring profusely when he had finished. Then he scrutinized his job to be assured of a satisfactory performance. Since he was content with his pursuit, he jumped into his red Ford Ranger and speedily drove to Hue's office. Assured of his mission, he sprang out of the truck with evidence between his bony fingers.

As Sammy entered the office, the secretary stared at him and blundered, "Ma-y I – I help you?"

"Yeah, like to see Dr. Dawson," Sammy said with confidence.

As the secretary scrutinized this thin bony man, she observed that he was wearing dirty overalls and was carrying a paper bag. She asked, "What is your name? May I ask?"

"Oh, it's Sammy Jones"

Sweet Peppers-Sour Grapes & Wild Flowers

As she thumbed through her appointment book, she announced to the strange looking fellow, "You don't seem to have an appointment with Dr. Dawson." Then she asked, "Is the Doctor expecting you?"

"He'll want to see me," stated Sammy with confidence.

Reluctantly, she pushed her intercom system and announced, "Dr. Dawson, there is a Sammy Jones here to see you."

Dr. Dawson enthusiastically answered, "Sure, send him right in."

Feeling as if he were a hypocritical betrayer, he stumbled into the office with his bag of bottles.

Delighted to see his yardman, Dr. Dawson smiled as he said, "Hi! Sammy! Good to see you today! What might be on your mind?"

Quickly displaying the whiskey bottles and explicitly explaining their origination, Sammy breathed a sigh of relief. Then he noticed the queer look on Dr. Dawson's face. He could not believe what his ears were hearing when the doctor spoke, "This is just a trivial matter. I would appreciate it if you would just dispose of the bottles and let this be between you and me."

Highly disappointed, Sammy slowly eased each bottle back into the bag and said, "Ok, Dr. Dawson. Anything you say." Then he turned and waddled out of the office.

Pastor Levi thought that he had discovered a strategic method to conceal his notorious habit. His intent was to remove the bottles and dispose of them daily. A few days had passed, and he had not executed his intentions. When he saw Sammy in the yard, he rushed outside to dispose of the bottles, but they had become invisible. Not remembering what he had done the last few days, he surmised that Sammy had made the discovery; however, there was no way that he could ask him. He would just have to keep an eye on him.

With great courage and strength, Sammy continued as a yardman at Hue's estate. It was noticeable that Pastor Levi had altered his attitude toward him, for he made unpredictable appearances in secluded places exhibiting some inebriation. Consequentially, Sammy had to inconspicuously look for bottles, but there were none to be found.

After a few days of pondering and giving much consideration to what Dr. Dawson had asked of him, *"Dispose of the bottles and forget about the matter,"* Sammy knew he had to make a firm decision. He was so frustrated that he decided to get Tom's opinion because he had great confidence in him. When he felt that it was the most optimal time for him to confer with Tom, he drove over to Tom's house on the spur of the moment. In an unperturbed manner, he lifted the bag of bottles out of his truck and carried them with him as he rang the doorbell.

Tom invited him in. Before greeting Tom, Sammy came out with "I was doing the yard work at Hue's house and minding my own business when I found these bottles on the lawn."

"Where on the lawn?" Tom quizzed.

Shuddering and quivering, Sammy recited, "Under the library window. You know Pastor Levi studies in the library."

Tom was becoming very anxious, "Will you repeat what you just said?"

Again Sammy articulated each word as best as he could, " Found these bottles on the lawn under the window of the library where the pastor studies. Been saving them for a few days."

Shaking his head with disgust, Tom uttered, "I am appalled at Carl, for at this moment, I will not say, '**Pastor**!' What a revolting development!"

An afternoon social was taking place at church. Tom decided that he would drive over and confront the pastor about the matter. When he arrived at the church, he met Joe Truss on the church grounds and concluded that he would just share it with him. Pastor Levi and other church members were standing on the church grounds also. Joe was all-ears, and unexpectedly, he headed straight over to Pastor Levi, "What's with the whiskey bottles that were found on the lawn under the library window?"

"What whiskey bottles?" echoed Pastor Levi.

"You know darn well what I'm talking about!" Joe snapped.

Again Pastor tried to circumvent the issue, "You, as always, are trying to stir up trouble. You are just a trouble maker!"

Joe grabbed Pastor Levi by the collar, looked him straight in the eyes and declared, "You scheming, cunning, deceiving scoundrel!"

Disdainfully, Pastor Levi pushed his hands away from his neck stating, "You holier-than-thou, over-zealous heathen! Only God can judge!"

The vociferous voices got everyone's attention. Joe lunged at Pastor Levi, as Tom reached them just in time to impede the jab that Joe was about to throw at the pastor. It took minimal effort to keep them apart because Pastor Levi was quite elated to have Tom come to the rescue and save him from this burly swarthy man.

Time passed; everything seemed somewhat peaceful; however, many members were disgruntled because of the lack of service that was being rendered by the minister.

Eventually, it was time for another board meeting. The President, Tom Best, called the meeting to order. Feeling very uncomfortable in the presence of Pastor Levi, Sammy, as secretary, inadvertently read the minutes from the last meeting. After approval, the officers were then called upon to deliver reports of decisions that they had been empowered to make. Afterward, the treasurer gave his report. Moving forward, the meeting progressed harmoniously in the proper order until Tom asked, "Is there any new business to come before the board?"

Without hesitation, Pastor Levi raised his hand. Tom recognized him, for he knew what Pastor was going to say because he had discussed the matter with him beforehand. First, he tried to persuade him to dispense of the idea, but when he insisted, Tom recommended that he should bring it to the board. Now here he stood nervously, about to make a motion, and he quickly said, "Mr. Chairman, I move that the board consider purchasing a laptop computer for my use."

Everyone anxiously waited for the call for discussion. No matter how eager they were to discuss, Tom leisurely stated the question clearly, so as to remove any doubt concerning the wording. Thus, allowing each member time to turn the statement over in his mind before speaking.

Ultimately, Tom called for discussion, and thus the interrogation began.

"Why would you need a laptop computer?" asked Sue Ann.

Sitting like a statue, he spoke with firm conviction, "I am totally committed to my work here at St. Luke. Composing my sermons could be easier if I had a laptop computer."

"Where would you use the laptop?" Joe inquired.

"At the house! The computer that I usually use belongs to Hue." Pastor murmured.

"Try coming to the office!" stated another board member.

Repudiation was expressed on all the board members' faces.

Waving her hands in gesture, Sue Ann tried to shame him, "You are being very inconsiderate of St. Luke!"

Things seemed to have been getting out of hand, so Tom called for the question, and a vote was taken. The majority opposed while Hue abstained. Joe promptly made a motion to adjourn. There was an immediate second from Sammy. Instantly, Tom stated, "Meeting adjourned."

Pastor Levi seemed to have been astounded by the outcome of the vote; wherein, he desired to continue the discussion; however, the meeting was officially closed. Trying to exonerate himself, he made an excruciatingly witty remark, "It seems to me that you all are trying to make me accountable. Well, this seems to be the best way to do it."

Kathy, Holly's daughter, who was the youngest and newest member and the only college student on the board, asked, "How would having a laptop computer make you accountable?"

"You see, I would use less time preparing my sermons; therefore, I could have more time for other Christian duties. You all seem to be squawking about my shirking my duties. I need more time," answered the pastor, arrogantly.

Looking irritated and slowly moving out of the room, Kathy expounded, "All that you are saying is irrelevant! It seems that you are evading my questions!"

The other board members had begun to ignore the conversation between Kathy and Pastor and were bidding each other, "good night".

Pastor Levi scurried out of the room while the other members gradually dispersed with the knowledge that the telephone was accessible for later comments.

Shaken and exacerbated by the seemingly unwavering board, the obstinate Sammy who had snooped into his private life, and the lambasting that he had taken from Joe, revengefully, Pastor Levi rushed to the office early the following morning to prepare his revengeful sermon.

Sweet Peppers-Sour Grapes & Wild Flowers

Holly noticed him as he swiftly came into the door. As usual, he didn't say a mumbling word. Approaching the computer with impetuous speed, he fiddled around for a while. From Holly's observation, it seemed that a bolt of lightning hit him instantaneously. Lickety-split, he grabbed the telephone and dialed a number. Holly's ears become gigantic sound pieces, as she overheard Pastor Levi, "Clara, do you feel up to coming to the church office?...Ok! ...I'll be right over to pick you up." He slammed the receiver down and strode out the door.

Now, Holly had just recently been hired as church secretary, for there had been a vacancy since Jonnie Mae Dawson passed away. With many laborious hours and perseverance, she had gotten the office back to its original exceptional condition.

In no time, he returned with Clara strolling behind him. *"They have the resemblance of a sly fox and a cunning cat,"* thought Holly. Sitting in front of the computer, the two tinkered and discussed, while Holly went about her work. This whole ordeal perplexed Holly, for never had she seen or heard of Pastor Levi and Clara working together on a sermon. *"Maybe this is going to be a masterpiece for Mother's Day,"* she imagined, *"for Sunday is a special day for all mothers."*

Chapter VII

The Sermon

On Mother's Day, Sunday, May 9th, the gorgeously bright sun rose on a perfect landscape of spring splendor. The May flowers were brighter than colored balloons beaming against the emerald green grass in most of the yards.

Most of the dignified, sophisticated, swarthy congregation at St. Luke dressed immaculately for the Sunday Church services. On this particular Sunday, which was Mother's Day, it was no different. Customarily, on Mother's Day, the offsprings worshipped with their parents. The children and grandchildren were all fashionably dressed. A female that had a surviving mother adorned her outfit with a red floral bouquet. On the other hand, a female that had a deceased mother adorned her outfit with a white floral bouquet. Mothers were anxious to be the recipient of a day of acknowledgement and recognition, and usually the tribute began at church on Sunday morning. Therefore, some of the members started arriving at 8:45 am, so that they could read the 'Prayer before Worship' that appeared on the program. Most of the parishioners were observant of the fact that the prayer alluded remotely to the forgiveness of the members' wrongdoings. Only the board members were able to interpret the underlying meaning.

Since it was such a beautiful spring day and also Mother's Day, St. Luke was almost brimming with people. Tom and Sarah's daughters were home from college, and they attentively sat by their beloved mother waiting for the Mother's Day sermon. The girls could remember when Pastor Trombone preached his Mother's Day sermons. He awakened blissful memories and continuously made them aware of how fortunate they were to be under the guidance of a Christian mother. Inasmuch as, they had grown up under Pastor Trombone's guidance and had fond memories of him, they were filled

Sweet Peppers-Sour Grapes & Wild Flowers

with anticipation on returning home and attending St. Luke. Besides, they were eagerly looking forward to hearing Pastor Levi for the first time.

As always, the service commenced at 9:00 am sharp. Whenever needed, Nellie played the organ. The parishioners at St. Luke attempted to sing the uncustomary 'Hymn of Invocation'. On the other hand, Pastor Levi sat stone-faced and did not make any effort to assist with the laborious task. Occurrences that followed were somewhat unfamiliar to the members. Unbeknown to the parishioners or board members, Pastor Levi had revised the Liturgy. The seasoned members had committed most of the Liturgy to memorization. Therefore, those who were reading were saying one thing, and those who had not discovered the change were saying the usual. Nevertheless, upon the discovery, some of the members were too stubborn to read what was on the program; they emphatically continued to repeat from memory.

When the preliminaries were completed, Pastor Levi rose, walked to the pulpit and took a sip of water from the cup that he placed behind the pulpit. Then he began in his usual murmuring voice, "As I was scrutinizing our church roster, a discovery was made. The discovery is that there is a 'Tator' family in St. Luke."

At this moment, Clara gracefully stood and strolled toward the pulpit as Pastor Levi handed her some papers. Everyone sat motionless, for one could not hear a pin drop.

Pastor Levi continued, "First, there is 'Dick Tator."

Clara held up a picture of a well dressed, paunchy, apple shaped man with one hand in his pocket and a cigar in his mouth.

Hesitating for a moment, Pastor continued to speak, "Dick Tator' feels that he is the most important of the Tators because he is the biggest hunk. He makes rules and regulations. He doesn't actually do much himself, but he has a voice LOUD enough to tell any other person what to do, and strangely enough, the person listens. Well folks, we do have a 'Dick Tator' in this church."

Oratorically, Pastor Levi went on, "Secondly, there is an 'Irri Tator' in this church."

Clara proudly held up a picture of a slender, scrawny man who wore a contemptuous expression on his face.

Continuing his sermon, Pastor Levi stated, "This person declares that he is a faithful worker, and he never misses anything; therefore, he has certain rights. He can arrive at most affairs fashionably late and begin lollygagging around, waving and talking to others while he is finding his place. He seems to say, *'After- all, I have belonged to this church for a long time, so I can do as I please.'* 'Irri Tator' has found out how to upset others, and he does it quite often. He seems to enjoy making others uncomfortable."

Getting another sip of water, Pastor Levi proceeded, "Within the crowd, there is 'Hesi Tator' who has second thoughts about everything."

Clara then presented a picture. The sample of 'Hesi Tator' was a stringy-haired fashionably dressed woman who had a stern look ingrained on her face.

"This person will reluctantly become the chairperson of a committee, and when she does, she will hesitate to call a meeting until she just has to. Therefore, the committee is not effective because everything is done helter-skelter! THINK! Are you 'Hesi Tator'?"

Taking a deep breath, and instantaneously looking at the audience, he read on, "In this particular place, we also have, 'Imi Tator.'"

Sorting out the correct picture, a few of them fell to the floor. Clara ignored them and quickly presented a picture of a fairly attractive looking man that was casually dressed.

Continuing his skillfully written sermon, Pastor continued reading, "Imi Tator doesn't like to be different. He doesn't make any decisions of his own. When others make them, he echoes them. When there is something to vote on, he goes with the majority. He never listens carefully; he stands when the group stands; he sits when the group sits. Whatever his friend puts into the collection plate, he puts the same. 'Imi Tator' just doesn't think for himself at ALL, for he's a phony."

By this time, some of the members and visitors became fidgety, some looked on in bewilderment while others began to scrutinize the congregation. The board members were aware of what had precipitated such a sarcastic sermon.

With a chuckle, Sammy whispered to Tom, "You must be 'Dick!'"

Tom nodded, "And you must be 'Imi!'"

"Think so?" Sammy whispered as he gave Tom a wink.

Meanwhile, Pastor Levi went on, "We also have 'Agi Tator.'"

With a tantalizing expression, Clara revealed 'Agi' who was a plump woman with a ruthless expression on her face. She held a hand up to her mouth as if she were whispering about someone.

"Agi Tator' is one of the family members who likes to keep things in an uproar. This member loves a lot of hoopla." Pastor Levi persisted as he wiped the heavy perspiration that was flowing from his forehead. "She knows all the latest gossip and is an expert at adding a little before passing it on. She picks other members of the congregation to pieces and I MEAN to pie-ces. Telling everything she hears is a real joy for her. She may not know people well enough to talk to them, but she knows them well enough to talk about them. Oh! The damage she does to people with that tongue causes much chaos!"

Many of the people in the congregation had become somewhat dispirited with the sermon, but no one moved, for each inquiring mind in the front of the church desired to hear the sermon to the end. On the other hand, those in the back were straining to hear and see.

To everyone that was capable of hearing him, Pastor Levi proclaimed, "Now, I will present the last member of the Tator family, 'Speck Tator"

Clara disclosed the last picture that she had retrieved from the floor. It was an illustration of a short, stubby, bald headed man who had a coward look on his face as he sat slumped in a chair.

The admonition was continued, "Speck Tator' gets to church early and goes right to his seat, so no one will notice if he is there or not. He just sits back and watches how things work. He never speaks at any meetings, for he seems to be in La La Land."

Pastor Levi glanced at his paper and exclaimed, "Now that was the last member of the Tator family; however, they have a cousin, and the cousin's name is 'Partissie Pator."

Proudly, Clara displayed a picture of an attractive, well-dressed young man who has a radiant smile on his face.

Pastor Levi strolled out from the pulpit for the first time where there was no microphone, stood beside Clara, and he expounded in his low rumbling voice, "Partissie Pator is an active church member. He participates in worship! Fellowship! Evangelism! and Service! He assists in strengthening Christian growth in church and community! How many of you can carry the name, 'Partissie Pator?" Pastor Levi then bowed his head and muttered a prayer that only those on the front row could comprehend.

Methodically, Clara gathered the pictures, handed them to Pastor Levi, and strolled to her seat in the back of the church while staring proudly ahead.

The overwhelming sermon ended, and the benediction was given. The organ music began for the singing of the closing hymn. Most of the people in the congregation made preparation for dismissal, for they did not attempt to sing the unfamiliar song that had been printed in the program. The hymnals had become null and void because Pastor Levi printed every word and action in the bulletin. This offended many of the parishioners.

Ushers strolled down the aisle to direct each row and also to collect the attendance cards. Members of the congregation solemnly marched to the rear of the church, trying not to pass the minister who positioned himself in his customary location while he reluctantly relinquished his weak handshake. They then gathered around in little football huddles whispering to each other. This kind of behavior was not unusual. Congregating in the rear of the church and discussing the services had become habitual for concerned members. This particular Sunday, the vast majority of the congregation wandered around in astonishment pursuing deliberation. Prior to this Sunday, Pastor Levi's sermons were unprepared, disjointed and incongruent. The members of the Board of Directors were aware that they had provoked him to finally prepare a sermon; or did Clara finally prepare a sermon?

Dramatic episodes were occurring so frequently since the new pastor had appeared on the scene, for it motivated the members to frequently discuss the late, Pastor Trombone.

Sarah expressed her weariness, "We appreciated Pastor Trombone when he was with us, but we never visioned that there could be such an extraordinary difference. When Pastor Trombone presented his sermon, we felt the Holy Spirit strengthening our faith, as he provided us with new freshness to continue throughout the week."

Trying not to be dispirited, Joe exclaimed, "Pastor Trombone possessed goodness, self-control, perseverance, Godliness, kindness and love. This fellow does not know anything about working through God's Word to obtain that kind of spirit."

"I guess not, for he doesn't seem to be capable of performing the God-given job," Sarah replied.

"I am curious." Nellie inquired, "Where did they get those pictures, for they were not fit for an audience. We could barely see them in the back."

Sarah spoke up, "Those pictures probably came off the computer."

"Oh, so that's where they mustered up those small pictures. We could not see them at all in the balcony, nor could we hear the sermon!" chirped Nellie in a musical tone. Whenever Nellie played the organ, she and the choir were in the balcony in the back where the organ was located.

"Well, you missed a treat; the pictures were hilarious, and the sermon was..."

Before Sarah could finish her statement, Nellie spied Clara standing on the wall alone as always. She surmised, *"Maybe, this is a good time to ask her about my money that I spent for her clothes."* Nellie gently maneuvered over to her side and was convinced that she was whispering, "Maybe we can work out a payment plan for the money you owe me for the clothes bought when we went shopping." A couple of the members turned around and looked, but then turned away.

Evidently, Clara had the assumption that Nellie could and would buy the minister's wife clothes. She stared in astonishment, and with her voluptuous cherry lips, she uttered, "Are you trying to collect from me because of the sermon that my husband preached? You KNOW that you are one of the 'Tator' members and you know which one!"

Astounded by this reply, a streak of rage flashed over Nellie, and she blared her eyes, pointed her finger in Clara's face and squawked, "Right now, I have several of those personalities, and furthermore, in the balcony, we could not hear your murmuring husband. All I want is my doggone money!"

Clara glanced around and discovered that people were listening. Like a pup with its tail tucked between its legs, Clara frantically scampered off through the seemingly hostile crowd. As she dashed for the restroom, perspiration glistened on her forehead, a lump was in her throat, and she felt a loss of equilibrium. As Clara glared in the mirror, she recalled how she always had to struggle for survival since she was a little girl. Being a very studious half White child, she was disliked by most of the Black students at school. Her mother, Vera, was Black, and her father, Stan, was White.

Vera told her the story of her conception. Vera was ill, and she paid a visit to the doctor, Stan. Stan pronounced that he had no cure for her illness in the office, but asked if she would meet him at his house not too far from the office. He would accommodate her with some medicine that he kept at his house. All the while he was thrusting a paper that contained his address between her beautiful brown fingers.

Vera was ailing with very little vim, vigor or vitality and had very little self-esteem; nonetheless, some hours later, she valiantly scooted over to look for the house. As her heart palpitated, she laboriously looked for the address that she held in her sweaty palms. She tapped her dainty knuckles on the door, and in an instant, Stan, with his wide alluring smile that exposed his creamy white teeth, announced, "Please come in."

Vera responded, "Thank you," and waltzed in the door. He politely asked her to have a seat and ingratiated her to the point of giving her an injection. Vera went limp as Stan carefully lifted her frail body on the bed and wasted no time getting to the nitty-gritty. Being in a twilight zone, she had no self-control or self-consciousness; however, she could tell when he removed her clothes, and when the intercourse was taking place.

Some months later, Vera, feeling like a nincompoop, informed Stan that she was pregnant, and that was the first time that she had had sex; therefore, she was sure he was the father. Stan immediately went into denial, and tried to muffle her with compensations. Being a very prudent person, Vera agreed to work with him on a confidential demilitarized zone while she tenaciously siphoned him for all she could obtain. Subsequently, Stan passed away in a freakish accident before Clara, his daughter, got acquainted with him, but she and Vera were left with some of his inheritance.

When she married Carl, she squandered her portion on him, and here she was – getting her clothes the roguish way.

Clara wiped her tears, powdered her face, and quietly exited the restroom to join Carl who had terminated his customary pose at the rear of the church and was alone in the study.

Goodness knows, the elegant Ms. Nellie Gray, with all her dignity and brilliance, was definitely out of character. With all the blaspheming with Clara, she felt lower than a snake's belly. For she had grown up in a Christian home with a very devout mother and father, and they certainly despised a foul mouth.

At an early age, Nellie expressed a musical talent that captured the attention of the church musician. She endowed little precocious Nellie with music lessons as soon as she possibly could. While her proud parents beheld the glory, she played for the Sunday school, church programs and other accessible activities.

On this particular day in May, Mother's Day, Nellie felt that she had succumbed to temptation, for she had resorted to profanity in the Lord's House. She departed the church calculating on just how she **WOULD** be reimbursed.

Chapter VIII

The Picnic

A pleasant breeze blew through Kingston and over Cherry Lane where the Levi family was residing. This made this Saturday afternoon a bit more comfortable. Carl and Clara never seemed to have very much time for fun with Kate and Kirk. Carl was always busy, and Clara was so much into herself that she did not offer many opportunities for a dialogue with the children.

Out of the blue, Carl announced that the family would be going on a picnic. Kate and Kirk were astonished, for they had not had a family outing in eons.

Carl Levi carefully packed a low-sugared lunch in his colorful German-made picnic basket. Generally, he disregarded the fact that he was a Type I diabetic, but occasionally, he would abide by his hyperglycemic diet. An immense amount of sugars and starches were inadvisable but greatly desirable, so he would administer his insulin and enjoy all of his starchy, sugary goodies. Today, he would comply with his medical recommendations, and he expected the family to endure the lunch without any objections.

Clara, Kate and Kirk were making preparations for the picnic. Carl called from the kitchen, "Are you all ready?"

"Just a minute!" Clara answered, "I'm trying to find a sun hat!"

"Be down in a minute!" yelled Kirk.

Kate silently meandered down the stairs and stood by the door, as she impatiently waited for the group to assemble.

Minutes later, Kirk leaped down the stairs and was ready to gibe with Kate. When he noticed that she wasn't in a gibing mood, he immediately abandoned the idea.

Nonchalantly, Clara came, joined the group downstairs, and the assemblage ambled down the road and over the hills until they came to a beautiful green spot that was sparkling with sun. As they spread out their blanket and laid out their food, everyone was chuckling except Kate.

Sweet Peppers-Sour Grapes & Wild Flowers

Kate sat in a rigid posture as she began to employ a Socratic format of probing questions. "Do you two have a tremendous feeling of accomplishment and satisfaction by bringing us to this spot on this date and forcing your bland food on us?"

Carl grappled for an answer, but instead he asked a question, "Don't you think that we should have some family fun sometimes? And for goodness sake! Shouldn't you be concerned about your father's health!!"

"Concern? Gee whiz! Why you don't seem to be that concerned about me! What about the expired time in my life?" Kate fired back with dauntless eyes. "You seem to be too busy for me, and it seems that most of the time, you are not concerned about your diet! As far as Mom is concerned, she seems to be almost incapacitated when she wants to be. Today seems to be one of her better days!!"

Clara interjected, "I spend lots of time with you at your school because of your controversial dilemma with your teachers."

"That's because I am armed with knowledge and can rise to the occasion when necessary," shrieked Kate.

Clara looked at Kate with pale eyes and morosely stated, "For crying out loud! Do you find that this is always necessary in all of your classes?"

"Yes! I challenge my teachers to step up to the plate and guide me on certain issues."

"When they try to guide you on certain issues, as I understand from Mr. Foxdale, you try in some way to belittle them."

Kate exclaimed, " That's not true, Clara!! You and the teachers are telling tales on me!! You all try to gang up on me!!"

Carl interrupted, "Mercy! Mercy me! I believe that students should be allowed to debate substantive issues."

"For heaven sakes, CARL!" Clara proclaimed, "There is a WAY to do it! Why don't you take time to go to school and handle this mess with Kate? And by the way, while we are on the subject, Kirk has his PROBLEMS too! Why, I am so-o-o **overwhelmed** with their school problems!"

While sucking on a lollipop, Kirk remained silent. Quiescently, he continued to lie on the grass and gaze up at the sun.

Carl stood up so that he could feel more authoritative. He gazed over at Kirk and inquired, "What is the problem with YOU – young man?"

Clara quickly announced in one breath, "He- seems- to- be - suffering from- a- paralyzing self-doubt- when- it- comes- to- academics."

Snatching and grabbing his beloved picnic basket and other picnic items, Carl roared, "Good heavens! Why did I have to learn about all this on a picnic outing? It's no wonder that I have a deteriorating heart and this devastating hyperglycemia!! Let's go home!"

Clara and Kirk retrieved the balance of the items and trailed behind Carl. Kate did not attempt to carry anything as she dawdled far behind.

Even though, they were twins, the Levi children were completely opposites. Kate was a high achiever with an overall "A" average; however, she was very authoritarian in her manner and attempted to boss others. This caused resentment and rejection from her peers. Kate also tried to get attention by demonstrating how bright she really was, and many times, she was antagonistic toward her teachers and parents. Of course, Carl and Clara felt that children should be expressive; however, kate had been allowed to do it with a belligerent attitude. The church members had become aware of her excruciating witty remarks to adults, and many of them avoided her.

On the other hand, Kirk had great potential, but he was carefree, and had an inordinate desire to be popular with the boys and girls at school. He associated with the bullies and other guys that would have loved to be suspended from school. About a week ago at a parent-teacher conference, Clara was informed of Kirk's academic and behavioral problems. She was aware that Kirk was on the verge of being suspended from the school, but she thought it might be advantageous to keep it from Carl since there were just a few weeks before the end of the school year. *"That was certainly a slip of the tongue at the picnic grounds,"* thought Clara.

Laboriously, walking uphill and downhill with the picnic basket in one hand and the thermos container in the other, Carl eventually reached the house.

He noticed Sammy toiling away in the yard. Carl's heart started palpitating, for he was trying to recall where he had stashed his

Sweet Peppers-Sour Grapes & Wild Flowers

bottles. His fears subsided somewhat when he suddenly glimpsed Hue from the distance. As he approached them, he greeted them with, "How are you?"

Sammy, stealthily, peered at Pastor Levi, "Good- good afternoon," and he proceeded to maneuver the soil around the plants. It appeared to Sammy that Hue's expression communicated a signal to Pastor Levi.

Huffing and puffing, Clara chirped, "We're fine! We're fine!" It was obvious to Sammy that she was fronting.

Trying to sound enthusiastic, Hue vocalized, "You must have been on a picnic."

"Yes, we were!" answered Clara very snappy.

"Such a beautiful spring day for a picnic – must have been lovely," Hue said as he followed Carl.

Again, very abruptly, Carl announced, "It was!"

Hue surmised that the Levi family's state of mind was not top-notch, so he decided to return to his office. As he was backing out of the driveway, he observed Kate dawdling up over the hill. From his observations, she was destined to become 'a thorn in the family's side'.

Carl went directly to the library, where he immediately observed that the trashcan had been disturbed, and his mail was opened. He was furious, for that was where he had begun stashing his bottles. *"O- oh my goodness! My mail! No one, and I mean not anyone should be searching through my mail!"* His thoughts were almost audible.

Carl dashed out the door and hastily walked over to Sammy. "Have you been in the library today?" he squawked at Sammy.

"No – no, Pastor Levi, I haven't," Sammy, answered very obediently.

"You wouldn't lie to me, would you?" Carl howled while staring Sammy straight in the eyes.

With a quivering voice, Sammy, very humbly, repeated, "No-no-no, Pastor." He then continued his yard work.

Feeling frustrated, Pastor Levi sauntered back into the house. He did not have the gall to tell Sammy why he had asked such questions.

As Carl scrutinized his mail, he realized that he must face the future with an undaunted spirit, and that meant more money. He was also cognizant of the fact that he had to accelerate the solution. Impulsively, he slipped out of his sweaty shirt and into a dry one, jumped into Hue's Volvo, and speedily drove to the church office.

When he arrived at the church office, Holly was there working on the Sunday's program. Pastor Levi had perused the program earlier, and she was shocked at his frantic unexpected return; however, she noticed that he was nervously searching through his desk. Eventually, he withdrew a piece of paper from the drawer that had scribbling on it, and he went to work with impetuous speed.

Holly observed Pastor Levi as he worked diligently at the computer. In the meantime, she went about her chores with exuberance, for she was in a blissful era. James had begun to attend church, and he assumed his job as usher, for his alcoholic problems had tapered. Holly was not aware of the fact that no one trusted him with the collection plate because he had been caught with his hands in the till.

It was getting late, and Holly had completed her chores, so she called to Pastor Levi, "I'm leaving! I'll see you tomorrow morning!"

Pastor Levi, urgently, yelled back, "Wait just a minute! There is something that I would like you to take a look at!"

Holly entered the office, and Pastor Levi handed her three sheets of paper, "This is a very serious matter. This will have to be taken care of right away; otherwise, St. Luke will be in trouble with the IRA." Holly was feeling very exhausted after a long day's work; however, she took the time to glance over the sheets. The summary of the papers was, *"He had a salary issue, and he was trying to show how the difference occurred. Percentages did not match with the resolution of the voters' assembly."* At the end of the last sheet, he made a threatening remark, *"It must be fixed by June 29th."*

Holly asked, "How did you discover this?"

"I started thinking and decided to work with figures," Pastor Levi declared.

Holly's thoughts were, *"He needs to be thrashed, for he is not performing a minister's duties at all."* Because of Holly's experiences, she felt that men mellowed from forcefulness. However, she pronounced in a pleasant tone, "Good Night, Pastor Levi, I must be on my way, for my husband is waiting for me to return home." She handed the sheets to the seemingly perturbed minister and glided out the door. Her home going was not as difficult as it had been years ago.

Holly's mind flashed back to some years ago when Pastor Trombone was still alive. James would come home drunk, and he would invariably find something to squabble about. She could remember one particular afternoon when he came home and did not care for the dinner that she had prepared. With a slurred voice, he muttered, "Whe-re did yo-ou git thi-s-s fo-o-od? It don taste go-o-d." He immediately started throwing food at Holly and the two children. Holly felt that the food would not do very much damage to them, but the instant James dashed to the cupboard, grabbed dishes and started hurling them, she knew that she should protect her children. As they dodged dishes, they swiftly vacated the premises and hid in the wooded area. In those days, there were few houses in the area.

When James stammered out of the house to look for them, he rumbled, "Wh-e-e-re are ya? I kn-ow ya out the-re so-me whe-re."

Very gently, Holly covered the children's mouths with her hands, while she covered them with her body like a mother hen.

When James could not locate them, he staggered back into the house, and vehemently pitched food out of the refrigerator. During his violent action, he muttered, "No go-od so and so; I'll fix yo-u."

Eyes protruding from the sockets, Holly crawled from under the bushes as a piece of the bush entangled her hair. She seized one child by the hand while she supported the other one in her arms. Her trail led her straight to Pastor Trombone's office, for he was always busy there in the day and part of the night. Frantically, she rushed into the office.

Calmly looking up from his work, he spoke in a very tranquil tone, "Please sit down for a moment, Holly, and we will talk." Pastor Trombone was aware of the Hollands' problem, for he had counseled them many times and had also made recommendations. In a quivering tone, Holly tearfully reiterated her story. Fearing repercussion if she were to return home, she asked to spend the night in the church office.

There, in the office, Holly and the two children slept soundly until they were gently awakened the next morning by Pastor Trombone. Then he escorted them home to assure their safety. Pastor Trombone seemed to have been so brave and bold; however, he did everything with prayer.

When they arrived at the house, James was sober and was standing erect on the front porch with a perplexed expression on his face when the car came into the driveway. He immediately scampered down the steps, dashed to the car, and as he opened the car door, he began to interrogate Holly, "Where have you been all night my wonderful lovely wife? Where are my babies? Why didn't you tell me that you were going to spend the night away from home?" At this moment, he seemed to have been an indestructible loving human being.

James' testimony was always a pack of transparent lies, and that made the matter more difficult for the minister, but no matter how much he was put to test, he never stopped trying.

After Pastor Trombone's death, Holly attended some self-help meetings and confided in one particular member. From this member, she began to believe that she had powers and unknown abilities. With those beliefs, she decided to stand up to James, and that is when the table was turned. She started switching him whenever he came home drunk. Holly felt that the thrashings that she rendered were not done out of malice, but hopefully, they would deter James' drinking habit.

Since Pastor Levi's arrival, Holly's attention had become divergent; wherefore, the abusiveness had somewhat dissipated. Tonight, it was her desire to have a peaceful night at home.

Chapter IX

The Hospitalizations

The refulgent moon was the setting for a romantic night. Radiant stars shone down across the dark sky as the pitter-patter of the raindrops composed musical sounds that assisted Tom and Sarah with their passionate lovemaking and later settling down for a sound tranquil sleep. Moments after they had elapsed into tranquility, the telephone rang. Making a great effort to bring his body functions out of its dormant state, Tom struggled to get to the telephone. When he finally retrieved it from where it rested on the floor, he uttered, "Hello-o."

From a distance came this desperate cry for help, "Tom! Tammy is sick, sick, and very sick!! Can you come?"

"Right now?" exclaimed Tom.

"Oh, Please, right now, and hurry!" Sue Ann replied.

Waking from a very titillating dream, Sarah overheard the conversation. Just as Tom leaped out of the bed, Sarah crawled out behind him. "I'll go with you," she announced in a wearied tone. Dressing like firemen who were on their way to put out a fire, the two took one glance in the mirror before they dashed out the door.

The glittering stars formed a shimmering pathway to Tammy Smith's dwelling that Tom and Sarah had been urgently summoned. There had been rumors that Tammy's reestablishment in Kingston was considered because of her failing health. Tonight, this was not gossip; this was reality. Plowing into the driveway and squeaking to a halt, the two rushed to Tammy's bedside. Taking one glance at Tammy, Tom suggested, "Call an ambulance right away!"

Sue Ann scrambled to the telephone and dialed for an ambulance because she realized that this was an emergency, and expeditious action was required. At this point in time, she was cognizant of the fact that her calling Tom was not overemphasizing the matter.

Fortunately, the ambulance came immediately. The attendants efficaciously asked questions about her circumstances at the time that she collapsed. They examined and inquired about all medications that

Tammy had consumed. Tammy was then put on the hospital cot and was wheeled out the door. Everything and everyone were so quiet that they could hear the breeze whisper, as Sue Ann and others whispered a silent prayer.

Having a great deal of concern for Tammy, Tom and Sarah trailed the ambulance to its destination. After hours of waiting, it was announced that it was crucial that Tammy be hospitalized, for the doctor's diagnosis indicated lung disease.

The next day, Tom called Pastor Levi who was at home as usual. "How are you, Pastor?" Tom inquired.

"Well, I'm doing fairly well, but I tried calling you last night about a very important concern."

With careful consideration, Tom responded, "Important concern!"

Pastor Levi proceeded at a deliberate pace, "I have a salary issue, and I'd like to show you how the difference occurred."

"This would be something that you would have to take to the Board of Directors. Our board meeting for this month is scheduled for next week. Can you wait until then?" Tom stated, while trying not to reveal his apathy.

Hesitating, Pastor Levi replied, "Wel-l-l, I guess so."

"By the way," Tom belatedly announced, "Tammy Smith is critical, for she was admitted to The Christ Baptist Hospital last night."

"Tam-my Smith. Is she the one that reunited with us after she returned from New York?" The Pastor asked.

"That's the one," replied Tom as he bobbed his head up and down. "And the diagnosis is lung disease."

Apathetically, the Pastor of St. Luke responded, "O-oh!"

"We suggest that you visit her," Tom interjected.

Pastor Levi paused; then he said, "Maybe you could go with me, she doesn't know me that well, and –and –and…"

Before he could go on, Tom interrupted, "I'll be there in a little while. Will you be ready to go?"

Reluctantly, he answered, "Yes, I guess so."

Very little interchange of thoughts took place as Tom and the Pastor rode to the hospital. Tom certainly wanted to avoid discussion of the salary, and he could sense that Pastor Levi desired to further deliberate. After the chit chat ride, Pastor trekked behind Tom as they

Sweet Peppers-Sour Grapes & Wild Flowers

went up the steps and headed for the information desk to assure them of their destination. A lady in pink who was standing behind the desk asked, "May I help you?"

"We are here to visit with Tammy Smith," spoke Tom in his deepest voice.

"Just a moment," the lady uttered as she thumbed through an index. "She's in room 204," and she handed them visitation passes.

Again, Pastor Levi trekked behind Tom as they proceeded on to the room. With a terrifying expression, he peered over Tom's shoulder as he stood in the doorway of Tammy's room. Tom motioned for him to enter the room.

The Pastor entered the room with his terrifying expression and goose pimples covering his arms.

Tom managed to bring him out of his stupor, as he spoke, "Why don't we say a prayer for Tammy?"

Strolling over alongside the bed, Pastor Levi stood erect with his belly protruding as he bowed his head and closed one eye. His prayer was protracted by his quoting verses after verses from the Bible. Yearning for a culmination to the prayer, Tom shifted from one foot to another. During the extended oration, Tammy groaningly reversed positions. Beneath her covers, alone in the bed with her head softly in the middle of the small pillow, she looked so dainty and helpless and seemingly incapacitated. She didn't seem to be aware that she had visitors.

Finally, there was an, "Amen". Upon completion, Pastor Levi turned and sauntered out of the room and out of the hospital. *"Obviously,"* thought Tom, *"He had visited a very few sick patients at the hospital."*

Observing the Pastor leisurely meandering around the front door of the house before entering, Tom was well aware that St. Luke had many more difficult days ahead. He placed his foot on the accelerator and drove in the direction of his home.

It was late in the afternoon on the next day that Tom received a call from Pastor Levi who reminded him of Clara's back surgery at the end of the week.

When Clara first arrived in Kingston, she was a recipient of numerous of ailments. Financial security and insurance coverage were obviously the reasons that Pastor Levi had accepted the position in Kingston. Now Clara had full coverage, and was taking full advantage of it.

On a misty Friday morning, Clara was admitted to Christ Baptist Hospital, and surgery was scheduled for the next day. The next four or five days, church members undertook many obligations with Sarah as the pacesetter.

Members dealt gently and leniently with Clara. Holly used her spare time to clean the house before her return home, so that she could save her of strain and discomfort.

Visitation at the hospital was superabundant each and every day. Nellie sustained herself with a visit, and even tolerated Clara's didactic conversation. Feelings were camouflaged by Nellie while she choked on her thoughts. When she felt that she was about to explode, she expeditiously excused herself and emerged from the hospital room. Perspiring immensely, she hotfooted it to her Mercedes and drove off.

There were some members, such as Sarah, Sue Ann, Joe Truss and Sammy, who brought all kinds of groceries to the residence. They felt that this act of kindness would relieve Clara some anxiety when she returned home from the hospital. With very little apprehension and reluctance, everyone ran to and fro to prepare for Clara's release.

After being a hospital occupant for a week, Clara returned home. She didn't call anyone, nor did she make any effort to thank anyone for any chores, performances or visitations.

In the meantime, some impulsive force seized Sarah's imagination; she could not resist the urge to visit Clara. Slipping her svelte figure into a trendy gold outfit, Sarah strolled over to Clara's residence. Being in topnotch shape, she delighted in walking, so she hummed as she leisurely walked along in the summer afternoon breeze. Being unsure of the kind of reception she would receive, a tinge of apprehension loomed in the pit of her stomach. Self-doubt had just about consumed her when she reached the house. Just as she was about to ring the doorbell, Pastor Levi opened the door.

"Good Evening, Pastor, How are you?"

"I'm Okay. Come on in!"

Sweet Peppers-Sour Grapes & Wild Flowers

As Sarah embarked upon the premises, she demurely stated, "I had not heard from Clara since her return from the hospital, so I decided to come over to see how she is doing."

Exhibiting a little exhaustion, Pastor Levi was not as loquacious this afternoon. He just gestured toward the living room.

As Sarah entered the room, she observed Clara staring into space as she sat on the comfortable plush sofa. She made a gesture toward a straight back chair, and Sarah reluctantly sat in the chair. Carefully choosing her words as not to mention any of the members' performances, Sarah inquired, " How are you feeling today?"

Clara was her usual complaining self, "My back hurts so much, for I am not sure when I will be able to be myself again. But, I am sure glad to return home. The habitation at the hospital was somewhat endurable. I guess I can say it was tolerable."

Once more, Sarah inquired, "What time did you return home yesterday?"

With a twist of her voluptuous lips, Clara gave a frown as her big brown eyes with all her curly eyelashes began eyeballing the ceiling, "Maybe ur-ur a-bout three-thirty yesterday afternoon."

"Is there anything that I can do to help today?" Sarah whispered while trying not to divulge her unwillingness. Sarah had many qualities, but she was far from being a nurse or a domestic helper. Her attire did not purpose to this kind of contribution.

Carefully scrutinizing Sarah's outfit, Clara lifted her head upright while she looked her straight in the eyes and proudly proclaimed, "My husband has been a Godsend for me today. I haven't had to want for anything because he made sure I had everything at my finger tips."

Feeling a sense of relief, Sarah sat erect as she crossed her long slender brown legs, "I am happy to hear that, for that is great." Trying to make an easy smooth exit, Sarah exclaimed, "I must return home before it gets dark outside."

Clara undertook no effort to detain her, as she straightforwardly replied, "Yes, it does seem to be getting dark outside."

With a compulsive urge to become invisible, Sarah said her "good-bye," and hastened out the door and down the walk and was on her way back to her dwelling on Burn Street. As she scurried along, she silently scolded herself for this visitation.

Incognizant of her trip home, Sarah stumbled in her house and with jittery fingers, she seized the telephone in her outstretched hand.

She dialed; the telephone rang, and a voice on the other end answered, "Hel-lo."

"Hi, this is Sarah. How are you Nellie?"

"Oh, I am fine today."

"Just gu-ess what! I visited Clara today!" Sarah's mind was overflowing, and she felt that her conversing with Nellie would be excellent therapy, so she continued. "Can yo-u believe that Clara never mentioned **any** of the work that we performed for her while she was in the hospital? She **didn't** ev-en give me any thanks for my visitation, and I was there about ev-ery day. Nor did she or Pastor inform us that she was returning home." Sarah finally stopped and took a breath of air.

Nellie did not interrupt Sarah, for she was aware that she needed to consult with someone. At this point, Nellie interjected, "That is just **hor-rible** for one to be so unappreciative. After **I** controlled my emotions and visited her. I even tolerated her meaningless chatter, for I knew that she was just trying to keep my mind off the money she owed me."

When Sarah was adversely affected, she would wend into tears. Whimperingly, she continued, "How could a person be so insensitive toward others? After all we tried so hard to make things comfortable for her when she returned home."

Nellie thought, "*I must try to console her to lessen the hurt. I do dislike Clara, but at a time like this, I must think of something other than calling her a dirty so-and-so.*" From somewhere in her soul, Nellie regurgitated what she had heard from someone a few months ago, " We are still trying to get to know Clara. You have given all that you can, so be thankful for your contribution, and you will be blessed."

"From the mouth of Tom!" Sarah expounded as she began to burst into laughter.

Chapter X

Another Service and Another Board Meeting

Telephones had served their purpose of transmitting information from one person to another in Kingston, Virginia. Talebearers, chatterboxes and busybodies jabbered incessantly for the past two days. By Sunday morning, just about every member at St. Luke had heard about Clara's unappreciative return home.

As Tom and Sarah arrived at church, Pastor Levi was arriving. Cognizant of the fact that he had a desire to discuss his financial situation, Tom scurried into church and attentively engaged himself in preparation for Sunday service. Clara's operation had impeded Pastor from having a one-on-one discussion with Tom; however, it was certain that it was imminent. Anyway, board meeting was scheduled for the next day.

The diminishing church attendance was perceptible as Pastor Levi took his place in the pulpit. Once more, a chitchatty disjointed sermon was presented, and it contained its usual adjectives. He referred to "kick butt" God, "la la land," "na na person" as he jabbered on and on.

James Holland was peacefully sleeping with a snore that vibrated his lips. The majority of the congregation was listening to James as his amplification almost overpowered the voice of the Pastor. With rigidity and intensity, Holly sat beside James and did not seem to acknowledge the fact that the sound was audible. Several of the members peered at James out of the corner of their eyes. No one would stare because it was rumored that Holly was me-a-an and didn't take any mess from anyone. Many of the members were aware of the switching that she had given James.

Sarah whispered to Tom, "Why doesn't she wake him?"

Tom answered, "How would I know?" Tom could be somewhat short at times when he felt that someone was asking him what he called, "a dumb question".

At the culmination of the service, James stood with the congregation, and he stretched and yawned as if to relax his body.

Everyone was full of exhilaration to see Tammy Smith, although an oxygen tank sustained her. Exhibiting a pleasant smile, she continually thanked everyone for being supportive; however, most members had received a thank you note from her the week after she returned home. Tammy quickly exited the church to return home, for she was exhausted from her very first outing.

Customarily, the Sunday church bulletin contained a note of appreciation from members who wanted to communicate their gratefulness for a particular reason to the congregation. Tammy Smith had enclosed a message of thanks to all the parishioners who had thought of her in any capacity during her period of convalescence. Whereas, there was no written expression of gratitude from Carl and Clara for the enormous good deeds that were performed by the members of St. Luke while Clara was recuperating from surgery.

As Sarah reached the rear of the church, Nellie and Holly approached her. Holly inquired, "Did anyone receive a "Thank You" in any form from Clara?"

"We don't think so," Sarah and Holly answered simultaneously.

"That is a shame, and I also noticed that there is nothing inserted in the bulletin," Sarah stated as she uttered a sigh and shook her head.

Trying to calculate the family's intentions, Nellie attributed to solving the puzzle, "Well, maybe next Sunday they will extend their appreciation in the church bulletin." On the other hand, Nellie commented, "I am so **sick** and **tired** of these disjointed inadequate sermons."

Sarah chimed in, "Really, I don't think that the selection of words that he sometimes uses is appropriate for church services."

"Most of our members are dissatisfied, for we **must** move beyond this predicament," Sue Ann stated as she momentarily joined the huddle.

On Monday evening at 6:00 pm, the board members promptly assembled. With his efficaciousness, Tom Best called the meeting to order. Moving on, Sammy, the secretary read his informal minutes. His minutes included a verbatim account of the last meeting proceedings. The essentials included kind of meeting, organization's name, date, place, presiding officer, time of opening, secretary, disposition of minutes, name of proposer, original motion, record of

Sweet Peppers-Sour Grapes & Wild Flowers

vote, final form of motion, time of closing and name of secretary. Silence prevailed as each member of the board exhibited a combative attitude. Tom then replied, "If there are no corrections, the minutes stand approved as read."

Determinable, Tom continued, "The treasurer will give the financial statement."

Joe stood erect with an expression of pugnaciousness as he recounted the treasurer's report. Following the conclusion, Joe asked, "Are there any questions? ...The report will be filed."

Tom called for the committee reports, and they were efficiently recounted. The written reports were handed to Sammy, the secretary.

Remembering the hullabaloo that took place in the last meeting, Tom quietly reminded himself that he should set an example of courtesy and should not forget that to control others, he must keep himself under control. Sometimes, Pastor Levi made it difficult to have self-control, and tonight there were telltale signs of inebriation. Without a doubt, tonight would reveal the real test of his efficiency as a presiding officer. Tom began, "The floor is now open for old business."

Pastor Levi declared, "Mr. Chairman, I mo-ve to reconsider the vote previously taken on the purchasing of the laptop com-computer."

Hue quickly replied, "I second the motion."

Tom announced, "It is too late to reconsider the vote previously taken. That previously was a month ago." Now since Pastor seemed to be so antagonistic tonight, Tom decided to sit as an impartial chairperson and let the board members take care of him.

Anyway, Joe Truss was willing and ready to attack Pastor Levi under any condition. With an antagonistic voice, he pointed his finger and exclaimed, "Evidently, you must have turned your hearing aid down or off when we **de-cisively** and **po-sitively** voted as a majority. **NO**! We will **not** purchase a laptop computer for YOU."

Even under this kind of pressure, Pastor continued to exhibit a belligerent attitude. With an air of arrogance, he proclaimed, "It's not that big of a deal, but I thought **you** people would be knowledgeable enough to understand."

"Knowledgeable enough to understand!! What do you mean? We are knowledgeable enough to know that you a shirking your duties and responsibilities, and it seems to me or us that you are here for what you can get." These were the words from the mouth of the young but intelligent Kathy.

Pastor Levi divulged his next intent, "You may drop the idea if you like; however, at the proper time, I will explain the fact that my salary is inaccurate, and I will expect an adjustment in the very near future."

Another board member exclaimed, "Proper time! You haven't done anything proper tonight!"

Suddenly Tom thought, "Enough is enough. We must abide by Colonel Roberts in his *Rules of Order*," and he stated, "If you listened to the reading of the minutes by the secretary, that is a done deal. Will you repeat that portion of the minutes, Sammy?"

In a self-sufficient manner, Sammy stood and read, "After discussion on the laptop computer and the motion carried, there were twelve opposed and one abstained. The motion was denied."

With reasonable confidence that things had to improve, "Tom called for new business. Tom knew the items of new business that required action, so he introduced them one at a time, and they were peacefully discussed and resolved. *"Hallelujah! Everything seemed to be simmering down,"* thought Tom.

Tom asked, "Is there further new business?"

Pastor Levi majestically raised his hand. Tom reluctantly recognized Pastor's hand, "Yes, Pastor Levi." Pastor scrutinized the group for a while. Impatiently, Tom repeated, "Pastor Carl Levi, do you have any new business?" Some of the board members gave him a look that could only come from Beelzebub.

Finally, Pastor Levi cleared his throat and announced, "I have a salary issue, and I will show how the difference occurred. Percentages do not match with the resolution of the voters' assembly. Therefore, you owe me money."

Each board member was well aware that this was going to be a painstaking crafty deliberation. The heated debate commenced when Joe made the first statement, "You don't deserve what you are receiving!! Months earlier we gave you an increase for your children's education. What in the **world** will you ask for next?"

Pastor Levi was terrified of Joe because he seemed to want to maneuver to battle, and he had proven it several times. Since board members surrounded him, he decided to demonstrate his undaunted desire by explaining the calculations that he held in his trembling hands. Perspiration was streaming down his face; his shirt was soaked to the bone, and his intoxicant seemed to have had an effect on his ability to think, but he felt determined to have his say. Sporadically, he spoke as he gave a fragmentary account, "According to the Constitution and Bylaws, ministerial salary should be $50,000.00 annually. After calculating the uh, uh statistical value established by deviation.... standard or norm, the value of the variation at which a relative or- or uh rah absolute maximum occurs in frequency distribution of uh random variable, there would be a shortage of $200.00 each month. Let's see uh, uh, I came on February 2nd, and this is June. I have served YOU ALL for uh rah four months; therefore, you owe me a balance of-of uh $800.00."

Pastor Levi frequently insinuated that he was more intelligent than the rest of the congregation. With persistent efforts to prove that most of the board members were ignorant, he deliberately divulged this equivocal presentation.

"Sammy usually suppressed his feelings, but all the shackles vanished from his lips, and suddenly he began to vocalize, "What in the world are you talking about?"

"Yo-o-u wouldn't understand," Pastor Levi remarked in a scornful tone.

Since the incident with the bottles, he had consistently treated Sammy with contempt. Unmistakable, Pastor Levi was very revengeful.

Sue Ann wasn't about to let Pastor get away with that vindictive remark spoken to her boyfriend; even though, she was aware of Pastor's present condition. She stood, shoved her chair back, put one hand on her hip and pointed at the pastor, "Yo- o-u wait just one cotton-picking minute!!! We have adjusted your schedule to fit your convenience, increased your salary, and when your wife was recuperating from her operation, we visited, cleaned and delivered groceries to **the** residence. You, my dear Pastor, haven't shown not one iota of appreciation. There were no 'Thank You's' – written or voiced. You should be ashamed." Embarrassed about her sudden outburst, Sue Ann unpretentiously pulled her chair out so she could have ample space to sit. As she observed the faces of some the board members, she discerned expressions of gratification.

"All I can say is ditto, ditto, ditto," echoed Kathy.

Perturbed by Pastor's slurred incomprehensible speech, Dr. Hue Dawson spoke up, "The report that you have submitted to us does not substantiate reimbursement of $800.00." Obviously, the other board members were stricken beyond belief. That was the first time that Hue had objected to anything Pastor had presented. Pastor Levi looked at Hue in disbelief.

Immediately, Hue announced, "Pastor has a written account of this report for you all."

Responsively, Pastor passed each member a sheet containing his calculations. Some of the members took a quick glance at it, and others sat passively without any observation. Joe destroyed his by ripping it into small pieces, and then blatantly disposing of it in the trashcan.

Tom definitely was not in favor of bestowing $800.00 to the Pastor. He felt that it was significant that he interject and explicate some of the things that had been expressed. " Pastor Levi, before the next meeting, I will take some time to meet with you, and we can see what has happened. Means, mode and deviation are explained explicitly on the sheet that you distributed; however, your deliberation was incomprehensible. Furthermore, those terms don't mean a 'hill of beans' to some of us. Many of us studied statistics in school, but we haven't had a chance to use it. Therefore, it has dissipated. To the members of the board- Please be careful how you vocalize or humiliate. At this time, will someone make a motion on the matter?"

Hue said, "Mr. Chairman, I move that we postpone the matter until our next meeting. That would give us ample time to substantiate the calculations."

"I second the motion," said Sue Ann.

The chairman then said, "It has been moved and seconded that the motion be postponed until our next meeting."

The meeting was adjourned with exhaustion and resentment. Joe definitely wanted the proposal out – never to be heard of again. As he strolled out the door, he grunted and grumbled, "Why didn't we just say 'no, no way drunken buddy' and be done with it?"

Chapter XI

Time of Bereavement

Shortly after Tom returned home from board meeting, he received a call that Tammy Smith has passed away. For the next week, the parishioners at St. Luke were in mourning, for they were deeply saddened by the death of Tammy Smith. Sue Ann did not contact Pastor Levi. In fact, she was hoping that he would not visit during the time of bereavement.

Pastor Levi did not express any sign of sorrow or grief. Even though, Tom had lost a cousin, he insisted on discussing the monetary matter with him. With determination, he telephoned Tom almost every day insisting that he give the matter immediate attention. Moreover, Tom reminded him that it was his duty to visit the family of a deceased parishioner.

The Smith family was very resentful toward Pastor because he insulted and offended some of the members of the family. Pastor Levi had experienced the effect of their resentfulness; consequently, he was reluctant to visit the home. He revealed to Tom that he would feel somewhat comfortable if he would accompany him to the residence.

One evening, Tom and Pastor Levi visited the family of Tammy Smith. When the two proceeded to enter the front door, Tom observed Sammy standing out by an oak tree. Tom made an impetuous pivot and headed toward Sammy. Pastor Levi went into the house unescorted. He stood reclusively by the door while everyone mingled. The family members behaved as if he were invisible. Nervously, he shifted his weight from one foot to the other. He was tired of standing, and no one acknowledged his presence. The aroma of the food, permeating the room, made him hungry. Suddenly, he began to feel dizzy, and his heart began to palpitate. He then remembered that he had not eaten for several hours, and he feared a hypoglycemic attack, so he decided to mosey over and sit in the dilapidated chair, located in the corner, until Tom appeared. As soon as he sat down, the chair crumbled to the floor. Two teenagers dashed over giggling as they assisted him to his feet. He stood and squirmed with embarrassment as one of them inquired, "What is your name?" He did not mumble a sound, and he scurried out the door as he heard a voice calling, "Pastor Levi! Pastor Levi!"

The voice reverberated in the air, as he advanced toward the parked cars. He felt that it would be expedient that he keep moving. Inasmuch as he was in a state of mental and physical torpor, it seemed that all the cars that were parked outside were similar. As he stumbled around searching for Tom's car, the cool air apprised him of the fact that he was wet with perspiration. It seemed like hours before he finally discovered Tom's car. He opened the door, jumped in and tried to become invisible.

Tom partially blocked out his conversation with Sammy as he observed Pastor Levi hustling out of the house and incoherently wandering around the parked cars. He noticed that he finally got into his car, slamming the door behind him. As far as Tom was concerned, his demeanor demonstrated anger. Suddenly changing the conversation, he exclaimed, "I wonder what went wrong in the house!"

Sammy squinted his eyes as he looked toward the car. Then he humped his shoulders and nonchalantly stated, "It's no telling, Tom, why it's no telling."

"I think I should go and check on Pastor Levi. I'll see you later!" Tom uttered as he made his way to the car.

Tom got in the car and looked over at Pastor Levi. He was as red as a beet and shaking like a leaf on a tree on a windy day. His hair was standing straight up on his head, and he was perspiring profusely.

Tom inquired, "What happened in the house?"

Pastor Levi stated, "Those were insolent people in that house! What they did was not very smart! This could institute a lawsuit! Well, I can't blame such people because…"

Tom decided to interrupt before he had said too much or gone too far, "Pray tell me! What did they do?"

"They planted a dilapidated chair in the corner for me to sit in! I fell for the scheme and almost **killed** myself! That can institute a lawsuit! Now you know, that was not very smart!" Pastor Levi reiterated.

Sweet Peppers-Sour Grapes & Wild Flowers

Trying to soothe the situation, Tom stated, "That old chair has been there for a while. I don't think that anyone would try to hurt you. I'll go by the house later on and make sure that the chair is thrown out, so that no one else will sit in it."

Suddenly, Pastor Levi remembered that he had not prepared the programs, and the funeral would take place in a couple of days. "I'll have to prepare the programs soon," Pastor stated in his dictatorship voice.

"Never mind; the family desires to prepare them, but I'm sure that they intend for you to render a sermon," Tom stated.

"Yes, I guess so," he said with a sunken expression. Then he spoke up, "I am extremely dissatisfied with the Smith family's conduct! They **must** execute the service according to **our** Constitution and Bylaws!"

Tom looked him in the eyes and announced, "Call them and tell them."

Pastor Levi hung his head and whispered, "I think I better leave it alone."

After Tom drove Pastor home, he returned to the Smith's residence to get an understanding of the nature of the alleged plot that the pastor had reported to him. When he walked in the living room, there was no broken chair to be seen. Therefore, he asked Sue Ann about the incident, and she seemed unaware of Pastor's presence.

Sarah appeared from another room. She reported that she got a glimpse of Pastor when he was hurrying down the sidewalk, and she called after him, but he did not acknowledge her at all. Tom decided to just forget about the dilemma.

The Smith family diligently prepared the program. Because of Tom's insistence, Pastor Levi was scheduled to give a sermon, but unbeknown to Tom, a Reverend Jukes would eulogize first.

On Friday evening, Tom called Pastor Levi while he was engrossed in a movie. Lately, it appeared to Tom that Pastor seemed to have been immersed in watching movies. Whenever he held a conversation with someone, he mentioned something about a movie. Many times, when he was attempting to preach a sermon, he would make reference of something in a movie.

When Tom called, Clara answered the telephone, "Hel-lo."

"Clara, this is Tom. How are you doing?" Tom replied.

"I'm fine, Tom. Would you like to speak to Carl?" asked Clara as if she were in a hurry.

Tom felt that he might be interrupting their dinner, so he thought he should apologize, "Why yes, if I'm not interrupting your dinner."

Right away, Clara sounded a little more cheery, "Why, no Tom. We ate a few hours ago. He's watching a movie, but he will be glad to talk with **you**."

Tom could hear her call, "Carl, Carl, Pick up the phone! It's Tom."

Carl put the movie on pause, as he picked up the telephone and answered in a businesslike manner, "How are you Mr. Best? What can I do for you?"

Tom cleared his throat and replied in his deep, husky voice, "Pastor Levi, I guess you are aware that this is the night of Tammy's wake. Are you going to execute the service tonight at the funeral home?"

"Well, ur, ur, the family may not want me to do a service," he exclaimed.

Resuming in his deep husky voice, Tom proclaimed, "You are the minister of St. Luke, and it is your constitutional duty to render an Omega service. Don't you think you should be more concerned about the welfare of the bereaved?"

In a very aloof tone, he asked, "What time is the wake?"

"Family hour is from 7:00 pm to 8:00 pm at Dunbar's Funeral Home. Will you be there?" Tom asked.

Presently, Pastor Levi could not think of a reasonable excuse, so he said, "I'll be there." However, he really did not intend to show up at the wake.

At 6:00 pm the movie concluded, so Pastor Levi had a change of heart.

Reluctantly, he began to dress for the wake. Just as he was on his way to the study to retrieve his Bible, Clara expressed a desire to join him. Since he loathed the idea of going, it was a pleasure to have Clara accompany him.

When Pastor Levi drove into the parking lot of the funeral home, Clara observed Nellie's burgundy Mercedes. She instantly became hysterical, "I can't go into the funeral home! Nellie is inside!"

Clara had mentioned the shopping incident to Carl, and he seemed unconcerned about the matter. Nonchalantly, he asked, "Why would you care about Nellie's whereabouts?"

"You know what happened between the two of us, and this is too close for comfort!" Clara exclaimed as she remained in place while Carl reluctantly dragged himself out of the car. Clara felt she could not face Nellie at this time. She would remain in the car as to not have an inquisition about repayment for the shopping spree.

Pastor Levi was filled with apprehension as he slowly walked across the parking lot and dreadfully entered the funeral home where he faced the inexplicable Smith family and guests. An uncanny silence pervaded the room when he entered. Impulsively, he opened his Bible to First Corinthians and began reading. When he was about to finish his second chapter, a clap of thunder reverberated through the room, and a sharp streak of lightning discharged in the atmosphere.

As Clara sat in the car in the pitch-dark parking lot, the booming thunder rumbled, and the sharp lightning flashed. Just as Clara came to the realization that the car was parked under a tree, a ball of lightning rolled down a branch of the tree, and the branch burst into a scintillating flame. The blazing branch plummeted onto the hood of the car where the ignited wood continued to burn. Clara became desperate, for she felt that she was caught between the devil and the deep blue sea. If she remained in the car, it was apparent that she would be consumed. On the other hand, if she made her escape, how far would she get before Nellie or one of her cronies would seize her out there in the darkness.

Just as she was foolishly contemplating, someone snatched the car door open, grabbed her by her arm and dragged her some distance away. When the person released her, her shoulder was aching from the abrupt jerk. As she turned her eyes toward the flame, the car exploded, and she could feel the excessive heat.

"What in the hell were you thinking about – sitting in a burning car?" The deep husky voice unquestionably belonged to Tom. Then he continued, "It's a good thing that Pastor Levi parked a good distance from the other cars. It appears to me that no one wanted to be near the tree."

Remaining in a horizontal position on the grass, Clara decided to remain silent. After a while, she slowly elevated herself to a vertical position and stood on her weak legs, for the entire ordeal had completely enervated her. Glancing around, she scarcely deciphered Tom, Sammy and his two sons by the dull lamppost.

Tom recognized the fact that Clara was perplexed, so he decided to try to communicate with her, "Sammy had to leave the funeral home early because he had to return his sons to their mother at a certain time. I followed him because I had a few things to discuss with him. As we were walking across the parking lot, a clap of thunder roared, and it was followed by a streak of intense lightning. Of course, I decided to return for shelter when I noticed a car on fire, and it resembled Hue's old Volvo. Several of the church members had mentioned beforehand that you were sitting in the car tonight. So I decided to check the car, and **there you were!"**

"Thank you, Tom," Clara uttered. That was the first time Tom had heard the word -'Thanks' from a member of the Levi family. *"Does one have to almost meet his Maker to repeat those simple words?"* He thought.

"Would you like to go inside?" Tom inquired.

"No, I would like to go home. Would you take me home? Would you go in and tell Carl that I am going?" Clara whispered as if she were about to expire.

"Ok, I'll have to inform Sarah, also," Tom stated. As he turned around to proceed toward the door, Pastor Levi rushed out and started for the car when he noticed the fire department hosing his only means of transportation.

"What in the world happened?" he asked as he gazed at the drenched residue.

"Our car was hit by lightning." Clara replied.

By that time, a crowd of people looked on with 'oohs!' and 'aahs!' Then a voice said, "Oh, my God!" Tom recognized Sarah's voice. He immediately located her and proceeded to comfort her.

Pastor Levi and Clara were so dumbfound that they stood motionless and speechless.

Tom looked at the two dumbfounded individuals and expressed just what they desired to hear, "I'll take you home, and tomorrow you may borrow my old Honda. We barely drive it anyway. Is that ok with you, Sarah?"

In time of distress, it would have been difficult for Sarah to have a negative attitude. So she said, "Ok! Fine with me!"

Pastor and Mrs. Carl Levi and Mr. and Mrs. Best clambered into Tom's Oldsmobile, and they drove home in silence.

Early Saturday morning before daybreak, Pastor Levi called Tom.

Tom was barely awake when he lifted the receiver, "Hello!"

Pastor made an effort to sound jovial, "This is Pastor! How are you this morning, Mr. Best?"

Now, Tom was very perceptive about the mood of Pastor, for he only referred to him as Mr. Best when there was a purpose. Tom replied without answering Pastor's question, "Good morning! What can I do for you this early morning?"

"I was wondering if I could get the car sometimes this morning if it's not too much trouble for you," Pastor stated in a businesslike tone.

Desiring to remind Pastor about the funeral, Tom said, "I hope that you are mindful of the fact that the funeral is at eleven this morning. I will pick you up in the Honda – uh – let's -say about ten fifteen, and you may keep the car until you purchase your car. I will get a ride home with Sarah."

Pastor attempted to make a vehement excuse, "I certainly do appreciate your letting me borrow the car for a while. I hate to do this, but that sudden mishap was quite unfortunate, and...."

Tom answered before he could finish, "That's ok, I will see you at ten fifteen." Then, he hung the phone up before Pastor Levi could say any more.

At 11:00 am, the bereaved family in black attire marched down the aisle. As Pastor Levi got in line to lead the procession, he glanced at the program, and he noticed an unfamiliar format. He observed that a Reverend Jukes was to speak before he did.

Pastor Levi took his seat in the pulpit. Of course, no other pastor was allowed in the pulpit other than the main pastor. Reverend Jukes sat in the front row neatly dressed in a black suit and shiny shoes.

The program went as planned with solos and many remarks from the audience. There were resounding 'Amen's', 'Praise the Lord' and 'Hallelujah's' while Reverend Jukes stood in front of the church and powerfully eulogized Sister Tammy Lee Smith. He reminisced about her trip to New York, and how the Lord wanted her to return to her earthly home before he called her to her final home in heaven. He depicted her Christian behavior and the smile that she carried on her face after she returned home. "God was getting her prepared for her journey," Reverend Jukes proclaimed. Oh! It seemed to have been a happy moment at St. Luke; however, the St. Luke members were not accustomed to the lively high-spirited sermons, so they sat quietly with maybe a nod or a toe tap.

When Reverend Jukes concluded his sermon, perspiration was dripping from his face as the audience waved their hands and stood with resounding "A-men, A-men, A-men, Praise the Lord!"

With a terrifying expression, Pastor Levi took his position at the pulpit. He opened his Bible; he commenced to reading, and he read Revelation: 20th Chapter. Immediately, at the conclusion of the chapter, the audience spoke a slightly audible, "Amen". Pastor Levi continued to read Revelation: 21st Chapter. At the conclusion, the audience responded with an "Amen, Amen" that suggested that the reading had ended. By this time, members from the St. Luke congregation had begun to squirm with embarrassment. With a sense of indignation, Pastor Levi resumed his reading without looking up. Everyone heard him announce "Chapter 22!" Something in Chapter 22 motivated a family member to become emotional, for she screamed and cried while two others held her down.

Tammy's sister from Ohio ran to the casket and began to open it as she exclaimed, "I'm going with my sister!" One of the ushers, James Holland, restrained her while she struggled vigorously. During the scuffle, the sister's wig popped off her head and landed on James' head draping his face. Consequently, James was unable to see. Realizing the difficulty he was encountering, another usher, Joe Truss, desperately tried to assist James, but James was twirling around so fast, it was difficult to remove the wig.

Sweet Peppers-Sour Grapes & Wild Flowers

At this point, Sue Ann and her brother decided to handle the situation. They rushed from their seats, carefully collected the wig, slid it on their sister's head and gently cuddled her while they softly whispered something in her ears. Gradually, she became calm. Whereby, the two offsprings assisted her back to her seat.

While all the commotion was in progress, no one could hear the Pastor reading. However, he retained his composure and continued reading as if the commotion were nonexistent. When everyone was under emotional control and serenity ensued, everyone heard the Pastor deliver, "....of the Lord Jesus be with all the saints. Amen. May Tammy **Rest in Peace.** May God be with you all. A-men." He then retreated to his seat. The remainder of the program was completed. The ministers lead the procession out of the church.

After the family returned from the interment, dinner was held in the banquet hall for the family and guests. Pastor Levi did not return to church, for he absconded to his residence. As of late, he and his family rarely socialized with the parishioners, and they seemed to discourage Kate and Kirk's association with the other children at St. Luke.

Now that the funeral was over, depression seemed to almost consume Sue Ann. She was very much aware that not only had she lost a sister, she had also lost a dear friend. Some time ago, she realized that Tammy was not a grouch. For she understood that Tammy was in failing health, and at first she did not accept it. With the assistance of family and friends, Tammy gained a great deal of self-assurance. Later, before she expired, there were rapturous praise and contentment for her.

Fortunately, Sue Ann had Sammy around to attempt to cheer her up. At the outset after the funeral, he insinuated the advantage of having a wife. One particular evening they were reminiscing when Sue Ann related to Sammy a memorable sermon that Pastor Trombone had delivered on a Sunday morning in 1991. She could remember the year because she associated it with the year that she was hired at the bank. Sue Ann recollected, "The title of that sermon sure was powerful! It was something about in-in-surance! Let-me-see." She put her head in her hands as she collected her thoughts.

Then she uttered a shriek, "Oh! I know! I know! It was- 'Marriage Insurance Policy for Christians."

Sammy then looked into Sue Ann's beautiful brown eyes, and with a melodious tone, he whispered, "I would like to have that insurance policy. Will you marry me?"

Sue Ann became all misty-eyed. She took a deep breath, and then answered, "Yes! Yes! I – I will!" Sue Ann was stupefied with happiness. Her brain was about to thaw, when Sammy kissed her and softly whispered in her ears, "I have loved you since I met you, but I was afraid of marriage. Watching you for the past week, as you humbly took on such weighty task, made me realize how much I needed you."

Sue Ann rested her head on Sammy's shoulder as she whispered, "I love you with every fiber of my being."

They held each other close. Then Sue Ann uttered, "Let's get married right after the week of Bible school."

Sammy chuckled, "Better yet, why don't we get married right **now**?" They both laughed heartily while they held each other close.

Chapter XII

Controversial Times

Last week bright yellow school buses delivered happy students home in the Kingston's neighborhood for the last day of school. Most of the students would be attending Vacation Bible School at St. Luke. Meanwhile, Sarah anticipated on beginning to make preparations for Bible School on the following week. Her tentative date to commence Vacation Bible School was July 8th; however, she had not conferred with Pastor Levi. She was confident because she had been Director of Vacation Bible School for the last ten years. In spite of Pastor Levi's exploitations, she was determined to manifest reverence for the pastor, so she decided to discuss her plans with him. She also felt obligated to invite him to her first preparation meeting on Monday at one-thirty in the afternoon at the church office. During her explanation, Pastor Levi exhibited signs of inattentiveness. As she was about to conclude, he seemed to become aware of her presence and began to vocalize. However, what he communicated astonished Sarah.

"Clara would like to assist you with Bible School. In fact, she would like to be the assistant director," stated Pastor Levi in an authoritative voice.

Trying to be cordial and trying to conceal her displeasure, Sarah became tight-lipped momentarily. Cautiously selecting her words, Sarah remarked, "Clara has not attended church since her surgery, and likewise, Kirk and Kate are not attending. Where are they?"

Pastor Levi exclaimed, "Kate and Kirk said that they don't like attending church because some of the children stared at them. Clara said that some of the children like to play in the twins' hair because they have "good hair", and she didn't like for that to be done. She feels that the only way to prevent it is to keep them away from **those** children."

At this point, Sarah was agitated, so she asked in a harsh tone, "What does this have to do with Clara's attending church?"

"Oh, she decided to remain home with them," stated Pastor as he attempted to give Sarah a comforting smile.

With a feeling of disgust, Sarah asked, "Are the kids coming to Bible School?"

"I'll ask them if they are coming," Pastor Levi answered in his haughty tone.

Sarah thought, "*I might as well go on now.*" She cleared her throat, placed one hand on a hip, pointed her finger straight at his nose and proceeded emphatically, "They are your dependents, and you should have the say-so of whether they are coming to church or Bible School, or are **you** afraid that the children might play in their so-called 'good hair?'"

Trying to strategically maneuver the whole situation, Pastor stated, "Oh, don't worry, Sarah, they will be coming to Vacation Bible School, and Clara will be in to assist you!" Instantaneously, he strolled off.

Now, the last thing in the world that Sarah wanted to happen was to have Clara as her assistant this summer. She could remember when she first accepted the director's position. Pastor Trombone was alive, and it was a joy to work under his directions. He exhibited care and love for all the willing workers and the numerous children who attended each summer. He assumed much of the responsibilities as a God-fearing caregiver and role model for the children entrusted in his care.

Unfortunately, Pastor Trombone was stricken by a heart attack. Sarah was able to carry on, because as a Good Shepherd, he had worked with her, and together they had structured a methodical organized program.

On the following Monday morning after Pastor Levi had spoken with Sarah, Clara sneaked to the office without consulting with Sarah. She held a surreptitious meeting with Holly informing her of all the changes that would transpire since she and Sarah would be working together. From her little notebook, it seemed that she and Sarah had made an appraisal of the merits and faults of the program. The merits were sparse, and the faults were multitudinous.

Expressing herself very scholarly, Clara articulated, "Vacation Bible School is a challenging task for us as directors, and in order for it to be successfully implemented, we **must** be organized. We are certainly going to revamp the antiquated program. We will be converting from a self-contained system to a departmental system. I will go to the art store today and purchase some art supplies for the art teacher."

In a didactic manner, Clara continued, "Today would be a good day for me to purchase art supplies. We decided not just hand out supplies, for we felt that each person has to be responsible. Therefore, we will have a sign out and in sheet with worker's names alphabetically listed, and items systematized according to grade levels. You may begin to formulate that sheet, Holly. What do you think about color-coding materials according to grade levels?"

"Sounds great!" Holly replied as she shrugged her shoulders. However, she was feeling overwhelmed with the apportionment, but she knew that she had plenty of time in that Pastor Levi had assumed full responsibility of Sundays' programs. Furthermore, she would not be a disputant, since Clara was demonstrating such decisiveness after meeting with Sarah. Holly continued, "What color should I use for each grade level?"

Continuing to employ her astuteness, Clara waved her hand, puckered her mouth and eyeballed the ceiling as she spoke, "Why Hol-ly, just use some bright colors; I'm sure you know how to do that."

Before she departed, she brazenly gave her the name of the starter's kit for Vacation Bible School that Clara insinuated that the two directors had selected. Continuing to exercise her authority, she demanded, "Holly, order that immediately."

Holly was not aware of the fact that Clara and Sarah had not collaborated. She detested Clara's authoritativeness, and she mumbled to herself, *"I don't understand why Sarah invited such a dictator to assist her, for I will have to talk with her about this. But before I call her, I will order the suggested starter's kit."*

First, Holly plunged headlong and completed the application for the starter's kit. With a sigh of relief, she dropped it in with the out mail just in time for the mail carrier, Gail, to collect it. Gail was a cheerful, efficient, businesslike mail carrier. She said a zingy, "Good Morning!" and asked, "How are you today, Holly?"

"Oh, I'm fine, for I have accomplished so much today. I even have my mail ready for you. I won't detain you today."

"No problem, I would pause for your mail any day. In fact, it gives me a chance to catch my breath. You know, it gets a little warm out this season of the year."

"Thanks Gail, you are an angel from above," quipped Holly.

As Gail walked briskly toward her car, she waved good-bye and said, "Have a good day, Dear." After fifteen years on the job, she was fully aware of the fact that her work demanded expeditious performance; therefore, she spent little time lollygagging.

Immediately after conversing with Gail, Holly began composing the sheets. She searched the cabinets for assorted colors of paper. She was so engrossed in her assignment that she did not hear Sarah when she entered. "Good Morn-ing! My! Are you busy!"

Instantly jerking her head around, Holly gave a sigh and stated, "Oh! You startled me! Well, Good Morning to you too."

Sarah asked, "What are you up to?"

"**That** lady**,** Clara, the one that you encouraged to assist you in Bible School, abruptly came in this morning and gave me the Vacation Bible School assignments. I guess the two of you are eager to get started."

"She-e-e gave you what?" Sarah inquired in astonishment.

"She came over with her black notebook, and I assumed that the two of you had collaborated. I should have called you before I listened to her."

"No, I have not heard from Clara. Pastor Levi tried to force her in on me on Sunday. To tell you the truth, I would rather not work with her. She is like a chameleon. She has the ability to change colors in different environments. And the **thought** of her coming over, without consulting me, infuriates me."

With eagerness, Holly supplied Sarah with every detail of Clara's visit. Sarah listened as she squirmed in the chair.

When Holly was finished, Sarah exploded, "That vicious little malicious character! She is going to strive to be a malignancy to our Bible School this summer, but I've got a surprise for her!"

Holly became very apologetic, "Oh, I am so-o-o-o sorry, Sarah. Now, I should have known that you were the authentic director. **That**

pastor put her up to this because he is so provocative. He should understand that we have enough work to do without trying to overcome this kind of aggravation."

Sarah felt that she had an arduous task on her hand; however, she desired to settle the matter as quickly and as painless as she possible could.

Reaching for the telephone, she asked, "May I use the telephone please?" She continued to be polite even under distressing circumstances. Carefully, she dialed; the telephone rang, and she heard the person on the other end answer, "Hello!"

"May I speak to Clara Levi, please?" Sarah asked as pleasantly as her flustered mind would allow.

"Who is it?" asked a voice.

Sarah swallowed to keep her composure, for it always irked her when someone on the other end of the telephone inquired in a tactless fashion, *"Who is it?"* She preferred, *"May I ask, who is calling?"* Sarah finally answered, "This is Sarah Best."

"She's resting and doesn't wish to be disturbed!" snapped Kate.

"Is this Kate?" Sarah questioned.

"Yes! Why?" Kate answered in her usual obstinate tone.

Silently counting to ten, *"1, 2, 3, 4, 5, 6, 7, 8, 9, 10,"* to help her maintain self-control, Sarah enunciated, "Kate, will- you -ask -your –mother, Clara, - to- call- the- office- or -Sarah- at- her- home- when- she- awakes?"

"Ok," Kate said abruptly and hung up.

Sarah had a feeling that Clara was trying to avoid her, and she was furious. Her temper flared as she decided to take direct action. In a stern voice, she asked Holly to call the book company and ask them to cancel the incoming order for the kit. Immediately, Sarah called another company and ordered the kit that she had intended to order.

Furthermore, she demanded, "Holly, you are to disregard all the other tasks that Clara has assigned, and you are absolutely, positively not to perform any duty that she ask if it is pertaining to Vacation Bible School. Just ask her to check with me for verification."

Holly was amazed, for she had **never** seen Sarah lose her temper. Seeing Sarah take control was gratifying to her. Especially, when Clara was the culprit. She was filled with exhilaration when she heard Sarah say, "Our Vacation Bible School will have the same structure that it had before. Classes **will** be self-contained because we do not have specialists to manage all departments. If she has bought supplies, it will come out of her pocket because no one asked her to go shopping for anything. Maybe, she will learn the hard way."

Still annoyed, Sarah departed the premises ready to share Clara's malicious behavior with someone.

Moments later, Sarah arrived at home where she found Tom preparing for board meeting. Hastily, she walked into the bedroom where he was dressing.

When Sarah appeared in the doorway, Tom surmised that something was out of kilter. Looking up, he inquired, "How was your first meeting?"

Shaking her head, Sarah replied, "You won't believe what happened today?"

Tom immediately stopped dressing and asked, "What happened? I don't have time for guessing."

Sitting on the bed to relax while relaying as much of the incident to Tom as possible, she began, "Pastor Levi was aware of my meeting with Holly at 1:30 this afternoon. I am sure he persuaded Clara to meet with Holly as soon as the office opened. She insinuated that we had conferred, and doing our collaboration, we decided on major changes in the Vacation Bible School Program this summer."

"What were some of the changes?" Tom inquired.

"She suggested that we discontinue our self-contained classes and initiate departmental classes, and much more, but you have to be going soon. I'll tell you more later."

"I am sure that Pastor Levi is behind all of this because he did mention that our Bible School Program was antiquated," Tom recalled.

"By the way," Sarah continued, "She presumptuously went shopping for art supplies. As far as I am concerned, that will be a donation to the Bible School. No one asked her to go shopping."

As Tom proceeded out the door to attend board meeting, he stated, "I'll speak to Pastor Levi about this matter tonight."

As Tom drove onto the church's parking lot, he noticed that *his* Honda, that Pastor Levi drove, was not there. With contentment,

Sweet Peppers-Sour Grapes & Wild Flowers

Pastor continued to drive Tom's Honda as if it were his possession, just as he drove Hue's Volvo. He made no attempt to make a vehicle purchase of his own. Customarily, he arrived at board meeting just on time, so that he would not have to communicate or socialize with the members.

On the other hand, the board members were accustomed to a few minutes of socializing before each meeting. Usually, they gathered early, so that they could drink coffee, eat cookies and enjoy the evening. It was delightful to know that Pastor would be entering just in the nick of time. Lately, the topic of their conversation was '*Pastor Carl Levi*'.

As Tom entered, the group had already begun the conversation. Joe had just begun his statement, "Pastor Levi does very little for the salary that we are paying him, yet he is asking for more."

"We should not give him anymore! He's not serviceable! He's not useful! He's not constructive, and certainly, he's not practical!" voiced Sue Ann.

Immediately, Joe spoke again, "He is doing more harm than good around here. It seems that he is trying to divide the church."

Docile, easygoing Sammy even commented, "It seems to me that no matter how ruthless he gets, Hue seems to be in his corner. There is something wrong there. Hue did not want me to expose those liquor bottles, but I *sure* did."

"I heard that he does a great deal of drinking! The only thing that he does for St. Luke is to hold the pulpit for a few minutes on Sunday morning because he **sure** can't preach. In fact, he is never prepared. I want to know, what else does he do?" were the words that came from Kathy.

"What- else- does- he- do?" two or three of the members reverberated at the same time. "He is determined to prepare the Sunday bulletin!"

Joe said, "You know why he does that! That is how he feels that he can control and manipulate us. I told you; that **man** is a DICTATOR!"

At this point in time, Sue Ann then mentioned some old business, "I can't get over the fact that no one from that family even bothered to say- 'Thank You!' – in any shape, form or fashion after **all** we did for them when Clara had surgery."

"That's not all, they didn't show any appreciation when we gave them the Installation dinner," Kathy reminded them.

Tom then recalled what Sarah had relayed to him just this afternoon, and he struck the table with his pencil, so that he could get everyone's attention. Silence permeated the room as Tom spoke, "Sarah, our Vacation Bible School Director, scheduled a meeting with Holly, the secretary, today. It seems to me that Clara got knowledge of the preparation and rushed over to Holly and made her own suggestions."

"Why did Holly listen to her?" two or three members asked in unison.

Tom then continued explaining, "You see, Holly assumed that Clara had conferred with Sarah. At least, that is what Clara insinuated. Anyway, Clara took it on her own to go shopping for art supplies."

"I bet you my bottom dollar that he will try to present those receipts to the board tonight," Joe stated with confidence.

"Well, we are to vote that down. We will tell him that just maybe his wife wanted to make a donation to Bible School," Tom chuckled.

Kathy wanted to reiterate what Tom had just stated, "We definitely shouldn't reimburse her. We have not seen her at church since…"

It was 6:00 pm because the time clock, Pastor Levi, had just entered the room. He rudely walked in and sat down without any form of greeting to the board members.

Tom announced, "Will the meeting please come to order?"

Joe swiftly spoke up, "No! No! And I will say –No- again! Our meeting **cannot** be called to order if our Pastor at St. Luke Church, namely **Pastor Carl Levi,** has not had the decency to greet us properly when he entered the room.…"

Before Joe could finish, Sue Ann chimed in, "That is so impolite and discourteous!"

Everyone turned and gazed at Pastor Levi while silence again permeated the room.

Pastor sat thumbing through his bible completely ignoring the penetrating eyes. Several sheets of paper protruded out of the pages. Everyone was aware that those papers were his reports for more money. He had obtained many nicknames, but the one that the board found most fitting was '**Moneygrubber**'.

It mattered little to Tom whether Pastor Levi spoke or not. So he continued with the meeting knowing that there was 'trouble in river city'.

Fifteen minutes had been wasted, as Tom again called the meeting to order.

Sammy read the minutes, and Hue entered just in time to give his report. Expeditiously as always, Tom called for committee reports, and they were reported without a hitch.

With reluctance, Tom announced, "The floor is now open for unfinished business."

Hue raised his hand, and Tom recognized his hand. He stated, "We postponed the salary adjustment for Pastor Levi at our last meeting. We would like to settle the matter tonight. In my opinion, there should be an adjustment, for we have deliberately calculated and found that he has been shortchanged."

Of course, after Hue made the statement, a debate ignited.

Joe expounded, "Pastor Levi has shortchanged us since he has been here, why can't we shortchange him?"

"We owe him the money, so we pay him the money!" Hue fired back.

"So now Pastor doesn't have to talk for himself, huh?" Joe asked.

Hue tried to explain, "I just want us to do what's right."

"Even though our Pastor is a poor example of what's right? His contributions are meager, and I am speaking of his tithing also. He's just a **moneygrubber!**" Joe almost yelled.

"You tell the truth, Joe!" Sue Ann expounded with a chuckle.

Nodding her head in agreement with Joe the entire time that he was speaking, Kathy decided to vocalize her thoughts, "Hue, it seems that you want us to do the proper or right thing, but you fail to expect that of your Pastor."

Sounding very pious, Hue stated, "God would love for all of us to do the right things."

Tom also felt that it was essential that Pastor Levi hear the unadulterated truth; therefore, he did not interrupt.

Finally, Hue stated, "Mr. Chairman, in order to get on with some more urgent matters, I move that we vote on this particular item.

The meeting was then placed back in the hands of Tom, the Chairman, who scratched his head and reached for the sheets that he had on the table. He distributed them and reluctantly stated, "As you can see, there was a shortage. We will vote on the reimbursement tonight."

The vote was taken by show of hands, and the majority voted to reimburse Pastor Levi.

After all the other unfinished business was acted upon, Tom asked, "Is there any new business?" Things went smoothly until the end. Pastor Levi raised his hand. The chairman recognized him.

Pastor removed some receipts from his Bible and presented them to the treasurer as he announced, "These are the receipts that show how much my wife incurred when she went shopping for art supplies for Vacation Bible School. She is asking the board to review them, so that she can be reimbursed."

Tom let Pastor's hand stay suspended with the receipts between his fingers, and he stated very firmly, "We will not discuss that tonight. I will discuss that with you privately."

Needless to say, Joe nodded his head and looked at Tom as if to say, *'I told you so'*.

Announcements were made, and then the hectic board meeting was adjourned.

Chapter XIII

Seeking Help

At St. Luke, there was a numerically shrinking of the congregation, and the morale had decreased among the faithful few. The unwavering board members were steadfast and were desperately trying to sustain the duration of an ineffective pastor. Unquestionably, a mediator was an essential. Convincing Pastor Levi to consider meeting with the Kingston Circuit Counselor was a monumental task. However, Tom had his way of making accomplishments that others found unattainable. He persuaded Pastor to meet with them; however, Pastor wanted it delayed for a couple of weeks, and Tom and the board agreed. Matter-of-fact, this would give Pastor John Elbert, the Circuit Counselor, ample time to schedule a meeting with them.

Persisting on scheming and conniving, Pastor Levi's objectives were to utilize this time to contrive and document some duties that he had performed.

It dawned on him that Holly had mentioned counseling for her and James. It seemed that James' alcoholism was once again escalating. Impulsively, he hustled to the office where he had not been all week. Holly had stated to the board members that, lately, Pastor Levi only visited the office each week for a few minutes to print the programs. Hence, Holly was surprised when he entered the office door displaying a cunning smile, "How are you this afternoon, Holly?"

Revealing indignation at his unpredictable attitude, Holly completely ignored his greeting, for she proceeded with her duties without saying a mumbling word. Generally, Pastor would make an uncommunicative entrance, and he remained mute until it was advantageous for him to speak. Today, she decided to beat him at his own game.

Attempting to use prudence in his approach, Pastor Levi cleared his throat as he spoke, "How are you and James getting along these days?"

Astonished to hear these concerned words emitted from the mouth of the Pastor, Holly could scarcely speak, "N –n –not, uh, too, good."

Feeling apprehensive, she continued, "I spoke to you a few weeks ago about counseling. Do you recall?"

Those words from Holly's mouth made Pastor less tense, for now he felt that he could get down to the business at hand, "Let's make an appointment for counseling as soon as **you** would like. When would you like to make an appointment?"

Pastor had caught Holly at a very vulnerable time. James had had an alcoholic relapse, and for the last few weeks, he had been preposterous. Becoming apprehensive, she had relinquished her method of trying to reform him. Anyway, she didn't seem to possess a fighting spirit these days. She felt desperate, and Pastor Levi seemed to be her only hope. "Just maybe, he **could** convert James," Holly thought, and then she spoke, "We'll try to meet with you tomorrow afternoon when James gets off from work – about six, I'll say. I think he will come. Will that be a good time for you?"

Flushed with pleasure and tickled pink, Pastor answered with exhilaration, "Oh, sure! Sure!" Then he skedaddled out the door.

Early the next morning Holly began her mission. Trying to get James to attend a counseling session was a difficult task. He was an egotistical man, and the thought of telling his business to someone else did not set well with him. James asked, "What will I get out of this?"

"I hope it will cause you to mend your ways," Holly snorted.

James looked at Holly in disgust and stated, "From what I have heard, the Pastor needs to mend his ways."

Almost on bending knees, Holly begged and pleaded, "Please! Please! James! Maybe this is the one thing he can do well. Let's give him a chance. Will you?"

Now, James was hardhearted, but Holly was getting next to him, and she finally persuaded him to go. "All right! All right! I'll go with you this afternoon. Now, don't expect me to behave like a child!"

All day Holly meditated and deliberated on her meeting with the Pastor. She had no knowledge of his doing any counseling since he had been at St. Luke. Also, she had heard that he also was an excessive drinker. Then, she rationalized to herself, "Maybe it will take a drunk to help a drunk." Furthermore, she could not conceive of

James being cooperative, for if he did, it would be a miracle. "But miracles do happen," she thought.

On the afternoon of the appointment, Pastor was punctual. At 5:45 pm, he was sure that he was well prepared, so he sat waiting with a presumptuous air. He felt that it was a great privilege to be in control. Besides, he knew he was a man of formidable erudition, and with his acquired knowledge, he imagined that he could acquaint the Hollands with facts, truths and principles of marriage. Furthermore, they were in need of someone who was conversant with the social institution under which a man and woman live as husband and wife by legal and religious commitments. As he continued to fantasize, he imagined that he would be so impressive that the Hollands would support him in pleading his case with the Circuit Counselor.

While Pastor Levi was daydreaming, Holly and James entered the office with composure. Pastor Levi sprang from his cushiony chair and extended his hand to James with his usual weak handshake. After a second thought, he followed it up with a similar devitalized handshake with Holly as he stated in a businesslike manner, "Will you please have a seat?"

Holly was so impressed. With a broad smile, she glanced at James. He refused to look at her and certainly didn't reciprocate her overspread smile.

Leaning back in his cushiony chair, Pastor pompously and officiously began the session, "Mr. Holland, Holly tells me that you have retrogressed when it comes to your drinking habit."

Pastor Levi's voice did not set well with James, and belligerence was aroused in him. His eyes blared as he spoke, "So Holly tells you our business! What have **I** told you?" He stood up and put his index finger on his chest while repeating, "**I, I** haven't told you a daggone thing!" Holly got up and gently guided him back to his seat.

With self-assurance, Pastor attempted to undertake the situation anew, "Mr. Holland, would you like to talk about your problem?"

"**My** problem? Would you like to talk about **your** problem? I heard that you had a problem!"

"We're not here to talk about my problem," Pastor said in his usual murmuring tone.

"**Man,** tell me, why not!" James exclaimed in a harsh tone.

Pastor felt that he was losing control, so someway, he had to regain his composure, "Now we aren't stupid; we know why you're here," Pastor uttered.

"Are you trying to call me stupid, **Man**? Are you crazy or what?" As James spoke, he sprang from his chair before Holly could impede his progress. Clenching his hands into fists, he rushed straight at Pastor Levi, as he screamed, "I **will wipe** this floor with you, **Man**!"

Pastor Levi jumped up before James could reach him, and he shoved his chair between the two of them, for he did not intend for it to go forward, but it did. When the coerced chair rolled toward James, it hit his big toe prodding the toenail upward. The pain was agonizing. He held his toe as he yelled, "I will kill you for this! I **will** kill you!" Faintly, he could hear Holly crying, "Stop it James! Stop it James! Don't say such things!"

Pastor Levi was fully aware that it would be chancy to remain in the room, so he decided to take the cowardly way out. Instantly, he ran out the door and headed for his car. Closing the door and locking it securely was the wisest thing he could have done. While he was nervously searching the ignition to insert the key, James started tugging at the car door. Ultimately, Pastor started the car and drove off slightly jerking James forward. As he peered in his rearview mirror, he glimpsed James hobbling along after the car. He could tell that he was emotionally expressing himself, and he was glad that his ears were out of distance.

Holly attempted to treat James' toes, but James insisted on visiting the emergency room. Holly surmised that he wanted documentation of the accident. She hesitantly escorted him to the emergency room while he pretentiously limped beside her. The preliminaries included extensive paperwork and numerous questions. The receptionist wanted to know if he had reported the perpetrator to the police. James stated, "No, since it is my minister, I'll just let it slide." The doctor on duty cleaned and bandaged the wound and announced that the minor injury would be ok in a few days.

When Holly and James returned home, James went straight to the telephone and dialed Pastor Levi's number. Pastor Levi had been jittery since the incident, but he suspected that he should answer the phone. He utilized his clergy voice, "Hello, Pastor Carl Levi speaking. May I be of service to you today?"

James shouted, "I am going to be of service to you! I am going to get you as soon as I can! You almost broke my doggone toe, and you are not going to get away with it!"

Pastor did not answer; he quickly hung up the phone.

James waited a while and dialed back. Pastor Levi theorized that Holly was calling to apologize for James' behavior. He reluctantly picked up the phone; this time he just said, "Hello!"

Sounding like a real villain, James said, "You had better watch your children and wife because I will...."

Once again Pastor hung up the phone.

James called back, but the line was busy. At this point, James was experiencing a wave of excitement; hence, he knew he would attempt another call later.

Pastor Levi called the police department, and in a few minutes, a police officer by the name of Doug Cray was dispatched to the scene. Officer Cray was unaware that someone else was residing at 1522 Cherry Lane other than Dr. Hue Dawson. Indecisively, he egressed from the patrol car, strolled to the door and rang the doorbell.

Pastor Levi, courteously, invited Officer Cray inside where he explained how he was the knight in shining armor when he was attempting to rescue Holly from her pugnacious husband by counseling them. Out of the blue the husband became belligerent toward him, and now he is threatening him on the phone. He stated that, "As a man of God, I possess sincere evangelistic concerns for my members." The report was recorded as Pastor recounted it. Somehow, he had amnesia when it came to the part about the injured toe. As Officer Cray departed, he assured Pastor Levi that they would speak to the alleged offender directly.

By this time, it was well into the night; therefore, Officer Doug Cray decided to delay his visit with James Holland until another day. After all, most of the policemen knew of James Holland. They felt that he would not hurt anyone. The policemen classified him as a drunken merrymaker.

After giving it more thought, Officer Cray decided to just forget about it, for it seemed to have been just a trivial matter. James was just in a temporary state in which his mental faculties were impaired. He would be ok tomorrow. In fact it seemed to have been one of those everyday things between acquaintances.

Pastor Levi was ill at ease and edgy, and with persistent efforts he could not sleep. He was cognizant of the fact that it was almost midnight, but he felt that it was imperative that he shared this with Tom. Giving the matter very little thought, he dialed Tom's number, but he only got the voice mail. When it was time for him to speak, he began, " Tom, I tried counseling Holly and James this afternoon. According to Holly, they were having marital problems because of his heavy drinking. Things seemed to have gone haywire before the session got underway. James made threatening gestures to me while we were inside the office. Holly was unable to control him. To tell you the truth, I don't know how she puts up with that man. He is **crazy**! Just plain **old nuts**! When I tried to vacate the premises, he chased after my car. After I returned home, he called me more than once and threatened me. I've called the police, and the officer seemed to be nonchalant about the matter. That man is **craz-z -y**! I need around the clock protection! Maybe you can help me with this matter! You can call me back. Please, call me!"

Tom called Pastor early the next morning and made an attempt to assure him that James was harmless. To relieve him of some of his anxiety, Tom promised that he would confer with James.

Tom drove over to James' residence to have a chat with him. James ostentatiously displayed his wounded toe, and indicated that it precipitated the use of a cane. From James' point of view, he had not yet received justice; however, he agreed that he would try to reach an amicable agreement with Pastor Levi. It was concluded that they meet with a third party present, and it was suggested that it would be an active board member. Tom felt that he had successfully worked out the solution to the problem, and there would be reconciliation between the two.

Tom reassured Pastor that he was out of harm's way. Consequently, Pastor assumed that he had some security, and now he could focus on other business. He must consider another duty to present at the upcoming meeting because he was somewhat dubious about listing the counseling session as a duty that he had performed. It was Pastor's responsibility to have a graduating Confirmation Class in June. This was understood when he accepted the call to St. Luke's

Church. It seemed that the Commission on Parish Education was desirous of an ongoing youth education; therefore, assistance was procured from another church of the same denominational affiliation. St. Luke's students were invited to begin their Confirmation Class at the conventional time. It was advantageous for some; however, some parents and students discovered that the time and location were inconvenient. Therefore, attendance was not up to par. When the prospect of a new minister surfaced, it was understood that the minister would assume his responsibilities at mid session, which coincided with his arrival. He shivered at the thought that they had only assembled twice, and very little was accomplished at those assemblies. "Maybe, that was sufficient for most of the students," he thought. Immediately, he located his roster, his Catechism and the booklets that contained the final examinations. When he had mentally settled on a date and time, he called each student to remind them of the examination for graduation. Happiness ensued when a parent answered the telephone because each one assumed that his child would graduate in the summer.

    A few days later, the twelve prospective graduating students promptly met with Pastor, wherein, he thoroughly reviewed the summary of the principles of the Christian Religion that was embodied in the Catechism, and he covered other information that he considered pertinent. Thereupon, he entertained questions; however, there were none. From his observation, the students seemed lackadaisical, but the test ensued. The students aggressively went through the test and completed it in no time. While the students waited, Pastor checked the booklets for results, and what he observed disturbed him greatly. The scores were substandard, for only two students had barely passed the test. He felt that some of the answers were ridiculous. He stared at them and said, "How dumb can you get? We had a thorough review! What is wrong with **you all**? Some of these answers are absurd! There will be **no** graduation!"

    The anxious students returned to their places of residence and reported the one sentence that made their parents furious. It was, "He called us dumb!"

    Before Pastor could reach his place of residence, several irate parents had called, and they asked specific questions and demanded precise answers. When Clara was unable to supply them with an answer, they inflicted her with vicious remarks.

Clara was in a flutter. She was considering not answering the phone anymore when Carl walked in the door. Clara exclaimed, "Oh, Carl! God knows that I'm glad you are at home to answer the phone! What happened at church?"

With a dejected expression, he replied, "**Goodness Gracious, Clara**! I gave the confirmation exam to the students, and they all failed except two. Now! I'll take over the phone situation."

"Those parents seem to be very angry with you, Carl!" Clara spouted.

"I should be able to handle it. When I give them a substantial explanation, they should understand," Carl muttered with a pretended calmness.

Clara decided to explain that it seemed to be more than just the testing, she began, "Carl, the parents are inquiring about...." The telephone rang. Pastor Levi arrogated himself the obligation of answering the telephone.

Lately, he only answered the phone with the greeting, "Hello!"

To his amazement, it was James Holland, "Hi there! Pastor Levi! You thought that it was not enough to damage my toe, did you? Now, you also flunked my two children in confirmation class!"

It had not dawned on Pastor that Annie and Billy were James' children. This was the last person that he would want to antagonize. Tom had acted as an intermediary in the toe predicament, and it was assumed that they had settled the dispute about the toe. Pastor uttered, "We have settled the dispute about the toe!"

James clamored, "The **hell** we have! I'm still under the doctor's care. My toe is important to me as yours is to you!"

Trying to keep calm, Pastor murmured, "I don't have to listen to this."

"Well, if you value your life, you'll listen! You flunked Annie and Billy, **my** doggone kids. Then you **also** called them **dumb! Man**, are you crazy or what?"

Slamming the phone down, Pastor yelled, "**Bye!**"

The phone rang again and again. Clara, Carl and the twins sat staring at the phone and contemplating on the next line of action. With a doubtful look, Carl asked Clara, "Should I try to get help from the police again?"

Sweet Peppers-Sour Grapes & Wild Flowers

Clara reminded him, "The policemen have not been sympathetic in the past. Why do you think that they have had a change of heart?"

By this time, Carl was pacing the floor. As he walked nervously back and forth across the floor, his hands were trembling, and he had sweaty palms. He could hear the pit-a-pat of his heart. He took a glance at the other members of his household. Clara was sitting in a quiescent state. He could tell by the quiver of Kate's lower lip that she was about to cry. Kirk was always like the warden, for he displayed an indissoluble attitude. Carl picked up the telephone as he announced to Clara, "That was a death threat! Maybe the police will react **this** time!"

The telephone rang. "Hello, this is Kingston's police station. Officer Bates speaking."

"Th-is, this is Pastor, uh -Carl Levi, I have called quite a few times about harassing calls. This call is even worse, it's-s-s a death threat."

"Do you know who is threatening you?" the officer inquired.

Pastor Levi was pleased that he was speaking to an officer whose name he did not recognize. "Maybe, **this** officer will be of some service," he thought. He began, "Yes, I do. It is Mr. James Holland. He lives at 4461 Tree Top Drive."

"Do you know this person?" asked Officer Bates.

"I do! He is a member at my church. He has threatened me before, and I have called a couple of times in the past. Officer! This seems to be much more serious! My wife is **upset**! My children are **nervous**! Would you come out tonight?"

Officer Bates said, "Pastor, uh-uh – Levee?"

Pastor corrected him, "My name's Levi! Pastor Carl Levi!"

"Well, Pastor Levi, we'll see what we can do. We are sort of short-handed tonight."

Altering his tactics, Pastor decided to use charisma; he stated in his most dignified voice, "The policemen here in Kingston are known as the best in the state, so I am sure you will take some time to come out and look into the matter."

"Well, maybe, but I'm not sure, Pastor Levee, we…"

Instantly, Pastor became enraged because of the officer's persistence in the mispronunciation of his name; he blurted out, "For Goodness sake! My name is **Levi**! You have been of no help to us in the past, and it seems that I am not going to get any tonight. I could get more assistance if I would call an out of town policeman, or better yet, an out of state policeman!"

Officer Bates calmly stated, "Why don't you try that Pastor Carl Levee?"

Pastor Levi slammed the telephone down on the officer. Whereby his thoughts were, "They think that I won't call again, but I **will**! Maybe, by faith, I'll get a concerned officer."

It seemed that the two students that had passed the confirmation exam were Sammy's sons, Herb and Andy. The mother, Cassie, who was an inactive member of St. Luke, insisted that her sons graduate. However, most of the communicant and active members of St. Luke maintained that all or none of the students should graduate. This development presented disharmony among the members. It was also another problem for the Board of Directors to handle. Since it was such a delicate matter, Tom suggested tabling it for the meeting with the Circuit Counselor.

In the course of time, Pastor John Elbert, Kingston Circuit Counselor, met with the Board of Directors and Pastor Levi, and he was the intermediary while the group discussed and debated. Pastor Levi shrewdly mentioned that he desired to counsel those members that were in need of consultation; however, it became hazardous. He recounted the ordeal he encountered with James and Holly. He then stated that he felt that the police was somewhat unconcerned.

Sue Ann questioned his ability to counsel anybody, "Pastor, how much counseling have you done?"

"Ms. Smith, I was very proficient in this in my method courses in college, and remember **you all** hired an unseasoned minister."

Joe Truss frankly stated, "As far as I am concerned, seasoned or unseasoned, you justly and rightly earned everything that happened to you."

Sammy Jones and some of the other board members were also apathetic.

In spite of most of the board members' apathy, Pastor Levi continued. He related how he made an endeavor to have a Confirmation graduating class this summer. Board members gasped as he stated, "The students seemed to be incapable. I guess it's because they are mostly illegitimate children. There is only one other

Sweet Peppers-Sour Grapes & Wild Flowers

group of children in church and my children that come from homes with married parents."

Sue asked, "Are you saying that illegitimate children are dumb?"

"No, I am not saying that; however, there is some correlation," Pastor muttered.

Shaking her head, Sue Ann stated, "I can't believe what I am hearing!"

Other board members stared at Pastor as if to say, "It's no use to try to argue the point."

Trying to bring the meeting back on track, Tom asked, "What do we suggest that we do about the graduating Confirmation class?"

After the group deliberated on the matter, Pastor Elbert suggested that the Confirmation class continue with efficiency, wherein, a later graduation date would be considered. Hopefully, all the students would be prepared for graduation at that appointed time.

The majority of the board members voted in favor of the suggestion that was described by the Kingston Circuit Counselor.

After that statement, Pastor Levi diverted from the problems at St. Luke and quoted incidents that were irrelevant to the church. He revealed that Clara and the twins were mistreated in a certain restaurant in the city. He stated that they refused to serve them because Clara was overweight, and Kate was somewhat cubby. It seemed that the waitress suggested a meal that Kate should select because of her plumpness. Also, at another restaurant, he had received mistreatment because of his ethnicity.

Tom had heard all this before, and he decided that Pastor had reiterated enough. To take some course of action with the relevant business, Tom interrupted, "Pastor Levi, this gibber sounds **so** childish. Furthermore, we are here to get solutions to our church related problems. Pastor Elbert, may we hear from you?"

Pastor Elbert was well aware of the problems at St. Luke, for he had been informed in a written statement from the Board of Directors. Pastor Elbert had aforesaid very little, and as he spoke, his innuendos reflected the fact that Pastor Levi had been having surreptitious meetings with him, which caused the board members to become somewhat suspicious of the Kingston Circuit Counselor. They also became aware of the reason Pastor Levi desired to delay the meeting, for it was his desire to accumulate some documentation of his attempted duties, but it seemed to have backfired on him.

Mary Flowers Carter

The Counselor concluded, "I would like to do a survey of the church members to get ideas. Here are the worksheets, Mr. Best; you are to return them to me when the forms are ready, and we will schedule another meeting to discuss the results and also make recommendations." He passed the worksheets to Tom and bowed his head and prayed a prayer that there would be harmony at St. Luke. At this point, the meeting was adjourned.

Chapter XIV

More Atypical Events

It was an extremely warm day when Mrs. Lillilou Cox, a retired schoolteacher, boarded a poorly air-conditioned greyhound bus in Galliston, Alabama. A few days earlier, Cassie, her only daughter, reported to her that some preacher there in Kingston, Virginia had said that her only two precious grandsons, Herb and Andy, were illegitimate, dumb students. And furthermore, they were the only two that had passed some church test, and he refused to graduate them.

Lillilou felt that Cassie was too easy-going, and that was the reason why she had not gotten a husband. Anyway, she would take care of business when she reached Kingston. According to her itinerary, it would take three days and nights to reach her destination, and she was already sweltering on the stuffy bus. Cassie had tried to persuade her to take an airplane, but she refused the opportunity. She quivered at the thought of being hoisted that high in the sky and moving through the air.

As Lillilou journeyed from Alabama through Georgia, South Carolina and North Carolina on her way to Virginia, exhaustion almost consumed her. Countless time, she wished that she had not been one of those old-fashioned dressers with her stockings, girdle, high heel shoes, and her cotton blend dress. Why, she envied every woman that was scantily dressed. She had definitely made her decision when the bus stopped in South Carolina.

The bus driver emphatically announced, "You will have fifteen minutes if you need to get off! It is now-ow," and he peered at his watch, "four fifteen, so please be back by four thirty!"

Shoving her way forward, Lillilou hastily departed the bus, and headed straight for the ladies restroom. She stripped off all of her garments except her cotton dress, thrust them in her bag, and pompously strutted back to the bus and assumed her seat. To relieve her aching feet, she kicked off her shoes and gave a sigh of relief.

After the three arduous days of traveling, she arrived in Virginia with swollen legs and feet, stiff neck and aching head and body. Her Cassie and her grandsons stood eagerly while waiting for her arrival. Gradually, the bus came to a complete stop. At that time she attempted to insert her feet in her shoes, but she found it impossible because her feet had swollen considerably. They resembled inflated balloons. Full of exhilaration, she egressed from the bus toting her shoes in her hands as she rushed to receive her hugs and kisses. As Cassie drove her to her house, Lilllilou reflected upon her past.

It was over fifty years ago when she was a little girl in Alabama. She lived with her parents in a shanty on a farm. Her unrelenting dream was to get married to a handsome man and move away from home. One day when she was picking strawberries, she spied a young man plowing the field next to the strawberry patch. Her desires drove her to keep watch on him for the next few days. One day, she worked up the courage to become visible; however, he didn't take notice of her. She strolled over and stood in front of the plow. The man said to the mule, "Whoa! Whoa!" The mule stopped. She batted her big brown eyes and said, "My name is Lillilou. What's yours?"

For a few minutes the figure stood mute. Wherein he then murmured, "Casey."

She danced off and chanted, "I'll see you around!"

The very next day, she got permission from her mother to invite Casey to dinner. She also concocted a story about how the two had been secretly courting. When she asked him to come to her house for dinner, Casey agreed with a nod.

On the day of the dinner, she put on her best dress and spent hours grooming her hair. An invitation to dinner suggested to the women folk that they were planning to marry. They all congratulated Casey while he gobbled down his food in silence. Casey seemed to have been ravenous for food, whereas, Lillilou was ravenous for affection.

Each day Lillilou went to the field to chat with Casey. The only words that Casey uttered were "Yes! No! Maybe! Ok! I'll be there!"

The neighborhood ladies planned the wedding, and they were married in the small church down the road. After the wedding, she and Casey left for Galliston, Alabama. A portion of her dream had been fulfilled, and she was bursting with happiness. Their sustenance was their wedding money until Lillilou found a job in the launderette.

Within a couple of weeks, Casey disappeared when he pretended that he was going job hunting. In that he was so uncommunicative most of the time, he was hardly missed. In fact he and Lillilou were almost strangers. After he had been absent for almost two months, Lillilou discovered that she was pregnant. Some months later, a beautiful girl was born, and she named her Cassie. Happiness consumed her as she built her life around Cassie. Of course there were some hard times, but …

Right then and there, Lillilou looked at Cassie and proclaimed, "**You** are the best thing that ever happened to me!" Then her mind reverted to the actual reason she was in Kingston, and she anxiously waited for Sunday to arrive so that she could set eyes on **that** Pastor Levi.

On Sunday morning Lillilou's feet were still swollen; therefore, she had to attend church in a pink dress, pink house slippers, and she carried her pink purse to match. She felt heavenly with her daughter, Cassie, and her beloved grandsons, Herb and Andy, accompanying her. Cassie had not attended St. Luke in years, but this Sunday, she honored her mother's wish.

Tom and Joe aspired to handle the worksheets, that Pastor Elbert had prepared for them in a very professional, businesslike manner, with no deviations from the rules. Only members would be given worksheets, and they were to be returned immediately to one of the two men. The board members felt that this was church business, not community business. In the past, St. Luke's members had kept their business to themselves, and Tom and Joe desired it to remain that way. They were not aware of the fact that Cassie had called her mother in Alabama and reported church business. However, they were knowledgeable of Cassie's reasons for venturing away from St. Luke.

It was about 14 years ago when the unwed Cassie became pregnant with Herb. Pastor Trombone had a consultation with Cassie and requested that she not partake of the Holy Communion until the birth of the baby; thereafter, they would follow the proper guidelines for reentrance. Pastor Trombone unswervingly spoke of fornication and adultery as a transgression of the Divine Law, whereas he would elucidate with Bible Scriptures. In spite of some criticism, he was steadfast, and in everyway he also practiced what he preached. Most of the parishioners were staunch supporters of Pastor Trombone.

In any case, Herb was born, and Cassie availed herself of the reentrance procedures. All went well until she became pregnant again with Andy. It seemed that she vanished into thin air. The parishioners had seen or heard very little of her until Sammy became an active member of St. Luke, and he started bringing Herb and Andy with him. In as much as they became very active with the youth group, he was interested in their becoming confirmed. Even Cassie had taken on somewhat a new attitude about St. Luke since the boys had shown such considerable interest.

This Sunday's service went as usual, for there were the tiresome songs and an uninteresting sermon. Lillilou yawned and fought back sleep the whole time. She thought, "Lord knows, I didn't take that stressful trip all the way from Alabama to hear such a boring sermon."

There was Clara sitting inexpressively in a corner seat in the back of the church with a basket beside her. In the basket were little envelopes. All during the service, Clara passed envelopes toward the front of the church. Members would pass them on as they read the names on them. The envelope had reached its destination when the intended recipient read his/her name. This was done until some of them were returned because of absenteeism. Of course, these were the thank you notes for the birthday party that was given in March.

Now Clara had been absent for a few Sundays, but Pastor began early on soliciting her assistance. He was cognizant of the fact that the positive responses on the worksheets would be sparse; therefore, he was desperately in need of her support. After listening to his plea, Clara could see that it was indisputable that she was indeed a needed participant. Now that she would be attending, she decided to distribute some thank you notes; however, she was not familiar with many of the members. Thus, sending notes down front would be her tactic.

When the service concluded, members were handed the worksheets. They were to complete them and return them to the ushers on the door. Pastor Levi stood beside the ushers with his usual sourpuss face and weak handshake. When it was Lillilou's turn to shake his hand, she shook his hand with an iron grip. Pastor was a stronger person than the elderly woman. He loosened the grip and snatched his hand away. Holding herself erect and staring straight in his eyes, she enunciated, "I **am** Mrs. Lillilou Cox from Galliston, Alabama. This is my daughter, Cassie, and these are my grandsons who are **illegitimate and dumb.**" Pastor's sourpuss expression was instantly transformed into a terrifying one. Lillilou continued, "I have grounds for a lawsuit, and don't think I won't utilize my rights. I can't understand why these parents haven't instituted a lawsuit before now because..."

Before she could finish, Pastor stepped backward, rushed down the aisle and disappeared into the first door in sight. He just wanted to get out of sight and hopefully out of that woman's mind.

Being very curious to know what was on the worksheets, Lillilou requested information about them. She thought that it might have had some connection with the test that her grandsons had taken. Herb and Andy were hunching her, "Grandma! That is not for you. You are not a member of St. Luke." All at once, Lillilou snatched a sheet. Joe snatched it back, and it tore in two pieces with a part remaining in Lillilou's hand. When Joe snatched the second piece, Lillilou raised her pink pocketbook to hit Joe. Just as the purse was about to descend on Joe's head, Herb and Andy encased her with their arms and escorted her out of church. As she was being lovingly escorted out the church door, she observed a lady scoot by her and scamper for her car. Whereupon, she asked her grandsons, "Who is that lady?"

Herb smiled and teasingly replied, "Oh, Grandma! You are so nosy!"

Andy chimed in, "That's Mrs. Levi! Pastor's wife!"

"I wonder why she's in such a hurry. She doesn't wait for her husband after church? She doesn't **stand by her** man?" Lillilou stated in an inquisitive tone.

Shaking his head, Herb repeated, "Grandma! Grandma!" As they proceeded to the car where Cassie was waiting.

Intimidated Clara Levi sat quiescently in the car desiring to become invisible. Mrs. Lillilou Cox had frightened her when she threatened to sue Pastor Levi. She felt that this might give the unpredictable Nellie an idea, and she could not mentally handle a lawsuit.

The wait seemed like hours when Clara finally glanced up and saw Carl coming toward the car. "Gracious sake!" She thought, "What took him so long?" It was such a pleasure to see him because the waiting was definitely a difficult task.

Pastor had been returning home directly after service; however, youth and adult Sunday School convened promptly after church service, and on certain occasions, fellowships were scheduled. The faithful few members at St. Luke had decided to persevere and conduct church activities as they had in the past when there was a vacancy.

After church, Tom and Joe counted the worksheets and perused each one. There were two members in the whole church that gave Pastor Levi a good rating. The remainder of the congregation gave him a failing grade, for they rated him as very poor. Of course, most members wanted to remain anonymous; therefore, they did not sign the sheets. Hence, they felt that they had more freedom for authentic comments. They commented on the fact that the Pastor attended very few of the committee meetings, church activities or social affairs. Some of the members stated that he was unfriendly and immature. Others stated that he was dogmatic, selfish and unappreciative. Many stated that he declined to work in the community, visit the sick and shut-in or even make a telephone call to the members that were confined at home or in hospitals. He was almost invisible at church other than Sunday morning service. A few parishioners wrote a comment about his wife, Clara. They stated that she almost never attended a church affair; however, there were times that she would remain in the car while Pastor darted in and out.

Back on Cherry Lane, Pastor and Mrs. Levi settled down for a Sunday evening of relaxation. Kate and Kirk were both visiting school friends. As Pastor was sipping a cool beer, he commented to Clara, "It was very generous of you to pull yourself together today and attend church just to accommodate me. I feel that your worksheet will be very essential. After all, it is anonymous. No one would know that you...."

Sweet Peppers-Sour Grapes & Wild Flowers

Pastor immediately discontinued his remarks, as he observed Clara's unnatural mannerisms. He stared at her as he spoke, "You did do a worksheet, didn't you?"

Since the worksheets were unsigned, Clara thought of pretending that she had completed one. Nevertheless, she decided to give a straightforward explanation, "I became frightened by that woman, and I fled to the car without completing a worksheet."

Now, Pastor was so engrossed in the outcome of the worksheets that he had forgotten about the lady from Alabama that had tried to break his hand. It took him a moment to recollect, and then he replied, "Oh! That lady from Alabama! I think she said that her name was a Lilli something. How did she frighten you?"

Clara's lower lip started quivering when she attempted to speak, but she managed to say, "She-e-e said that she-e-e was going to sue-ue you. I was afraid that Nell-Nellie had overheard, and that would give her an ide-ea." As she spoke, she seemed to have been gaining her composure, and she continued, " The thought of a lawsuit terrifies me. I guess it is because my mother went through so many lawsuits after my daddy's death. I was not old enough to remember them, but by the way my mother explained them, they were troublesome."

Carl regretted that he had even brought up the subject. If he had kept quiet about it, Clara would not have had to expose her propensity of such feelings about lawsuits. Tenderly, he said, "That's ok if you didn't complete a worksheet. I'm sure things will work out. And furthermore, you don't have to attend St. Luke anymore. If that is what you want."

Feeling very inadequate about her mental health, Clara muttered, "I still would like to assist with Bible School. By the way! Did you get a reimbursement for the money I spent for the art supplies?"

"Tom and I discussed it somewhat. Say! Why don't you speak to Sarah about it?"

"No way!" thought Clara. "I might have to disclose some of my magnificent Bible School ideas to her before the appointed time." Whatever way, Clara was determined that she was going to be the director. She found Sarah to be docile and easygoing. Also Clara felt activated when she heard that Nellie would be on vacation the week of Bible School. Hence, she felt that this was an opportune time to exhibit her expertise in biblical education.

It was true that Sarah **was** obliging much of the time, but under the circumstances, the St. Luke ladies who had previously worked for the Bible School were not going to accept Clara as their director. Besides, Holly was an instigator who was working with Sarah to alleviate, or, if possible, eliminate all of Clara's duties.

As Carl turned and looked at Clara, he surmised from her expression that for the moment she was feeling a sense of relief, whereas, he delighted in knowing that he was the effective aid. For he was always happy when he could lend her a helping hand because she was so mentally fragile. Someway, he had to relieve her from this stressful situation. Just then a concept developed in his mind, and he began to ask himself, "What is desirable for us, or what ought to be?" At that moment he began composing a letter to the congregation, which he would insert in the Sunday's bulletin.

The following week, Sarah continued her preparations for Bible School. The group planned a luncheon with a food donation from each participant. It was her request that Pastor Levi would attend the final meeting to in-service the helpers on the lessons for the week. Pastor had the teacher's guide in his possession for a few days, yet on the morning of the in-service, he entered the room toting only a food contribution. Pastor Levi was boastful of his stollen. He happily explained to the group that stollen was sweetened German bread made from raised dough with nuts, raisins and citron. When he began the in-service, he was lacking of his teacher's guide and other instructional materials.

Sarah reluctantly provided Pastor with her guide, a pencil and a sheet of paper. He was **definitely** unprepared. Now, Sarah felt that it was not her duty to advise him on how to conduct a workshop. It was her intentions that he would study the lessons and have some method to furnish information that would encourage the participants to discuss, consider and examine the content of the lessons. The participants sat eagerly while trying to grasp the meaning of the lecture. He didn't seem to have a clue of the theme of the Vacation Bible School lessons; even though, there was a poster with vivid artwork of footprints within view, and on it was: **"LET'S FOLLOW JESUS."**

Sweet Peppers-Sour Grapes & Wild Flowers

When the workshop finally concluded, Pastor repeated a brief prayer and immediately made his departure.

With a feeling of exoneration, the uninformed group commenced to chit chatting while they enjoyed the delectable luncheon.

Joe teasingly asked Sarah, "Why didn't you prepare **your** Pastor for this workshop?"

Sarah chuckled as she replied, "I sure thought he would be prepared. You know, I **should** have given him a crash course on how to conduct a workshop."

Then Sue Ann interrupted, "Did you all know that Clara was sitting in the car while the alleged workshop was being conducted?"

"She was!" said several of the members in unison.

With an expression of disbelief, Sarah exclaimed, "You've got to be kidding!"

"You know she has a mental condition," stated Nellie. "I could tell you a few things. But!"

"I heard about the shopping trip. It's no use in trying to keep it a secret," chimed Holly.

At this point and time, Tom and Joe concluded their conferencing, and Joe whistled for the group's attention. Everyone seemed to have been considerate and gave full attention, "We would like to make a suggestion," shouted Joe. "Since most of the participants are here today, why don't we spend a few minutes summarizing the lessons? Sarah! Would you please do that for us?"

"Are you sure that you are prepared?" Holly chuckled.

"Yes, I am prepared, if you don't mind spending a few minutes, I will supply you with a brief treatment."

Some gave the suggestion serious consideration and decided to leave. While others graciously sat around the table while Sarah gave a compendium of the Bible School lessons. Then those tenacious members departed with some knowledge of the summer lessons.

Clara, in all her glory, was not aware of the session that took place in the aftermath. She assumed that the members were unfamiliar with the lessons unless they studied them themselves. Therefore, when Bible School begins, that would be the time for her to display her profound knowledge of the Bible School subject matter. Subsequently, at St. Luke she would be known as an erudite woman, and **just maybe**, she would have the stamina for continuance at St. Luke.

Now, most of the Vacation Bible School helpers were employed, and their time was limited for volunteer work. However, many of them felt that it was their obligation to help support their church with Bible School. As a rule, only the teachers and assistants had possession of a bible book anyway. To save time, in the past they had depended on Pastor Trombone's workshops, and during the vacancy, they assembled for discussions and deliberation. Hence, the week of Vacation Bible School at St. Luke had always been successful.

In the cool of the afternoon when Tom was just returning home from work, and Sarah was on her way in from working with Bible School, the telephone rang. Sarah got to it first, and Tom heard Sarah announcing, "Just hold on. He's coming in the door now." Tom walked in the family room when Sarah handed him the telephone. He reached for the receiver as he said, "Thank you, Sweetheart," and he kissed Sarah before speaking to the person on the phone. As he sat in his lazy boy, he said, "Hello!"

"Good evening, Mr. Best! How are you? This is Pastor Elbert."

"I'm fine, Pastor Elbert! I had just walked in the house," Tom replied as he tugged at his necktie until it came loose, and then he unbuttoned his shirt with a sigh of relief.

"I am calling to set up a meeting with the board and Pastor Levi, so that we could review the results of the worksheets. I was thinking of Wednesday evening of this week at my church. Would you be free on Wednesday?" Pastor asked.

Kicking off his shoes and continuing to undress, Tom thought, and then he remembered that he had a standing activity on Wednesday evenings. Therefore, he replied, "That's not a good day for me. What about Thursday evening? Let's say, about six?"

Pastor Elbert replied, "Let me take a look at my calendar. Let's see here. Thursday evening at six, uh. I guess I can move this appointment to another day. Yes, that would be good for me. After you check with the others, will you get back with me?"

"Ok, Pastor. I'll do that as soon as possible," Tom stated.

"Thank you, and I'll look to hear from you soon," said Pastor Elbert as he hung up.

Immediately after dinner Tom called each of the board members and Pastor Levi. If they were not at home, he left a message. The consensus of the members was that they would meet on Thursday at six, and it seemed that they would have a quorum.

Tom called Pastor Elbert and confirmed the meeting for Thursday evening at six o'clock.

Chapter XV

Vacation Bible School

Temperatures were soaring each day in Kingston to about 98 degrees. A breeze infrequently passed. The sweltering conditions forced everyone inside and necessitated air-condition. No matter how sultry the weather, the St. Luke members were full of exhilaration on Monday, the first day of Vacation Bible School.

It was also a pleasure to welcome Betty Trombone back for a visit. After the death of Pastor Trombone, she relocated to Ohio to be near her daughter and family. When she heard that Nellie would be out of town, she informed Sarah that she would be in town the week of Bible School and would substitute as the musician.

The Bible School was graced with St. Luke's active and inactive members as volunteers. The registrars sat behind the tables while the students from the community and around town lined up to enroll in Bible School. Kate and Kirk were in the crowd. Kirk wore a smile on his face; whereas, Kate maintained her unhappy expression. They were delighted to enroll this enormous group of children.

Registration had not been completed when it was time for the students to move to opening service with Pastor Levi. Since the large group was so overwhelming, there was an alteration of the procedures for registration. It was suggested that the registrars give each student an application, and the student would return it later. Those students that needed assistance could obtain it from the teachers or the teachers' helpers. The parents were then free to move on to their daily occupations.

Up in the sanctuary, the opening session had begun under Pastor Levi's leadership. It seemed as if the students were enjoying Pastor Levi. The laborious workers could hear laughter from afar, as they busied themselves for the children's return.

Clara Levi entered the room dressed in an exquisite olive-green silk short set with olive-green sandals to match. Ignoring everyone

Sweet Peppers-Sour Grapes & Wild Flowers

else in the room, she promenaded over to Sarah. Sarah was so engrossed in decorating the bulletin board that she was not aware of Clara's presence. A bright cheery entranceway was her desire. When Sarah spun around, she stepped on Clara's foot, "Oh, I'm sorry! I didn't know that you were here!"

"That's perfectly ok!" Clara articulated. "I came to bring you the guidelines for Bible School for this week." She then handed Sarah some papers.

Sarah reluctantly took them, held them in one hand, as she placed her last piece of design on the bulletin board. Clara hung around in the immediate vicinity. Then Sarah moved toward her desk, and Clara crept behind her. Just as Sarah placed the papers on the desk, Holly walked over, retrieved them and dropped them in the trashcan while Clara looked on. Clara then inched very close to Sarah and whispered, "I can help. I'm familiar with the lessons for the entire week." Silence permeated the room because everyone was inconspicuously observing Clara. It was not unusual for Clara to act mysterious; nevertheless, it was still intriguing to most of the church members.

Clara moseyed to the corner of the room and sat motionless. Sarah felt tremendous sympathy for Clara, although she was aware that surrendering to Clara would cause a complete devastation of the week of Bible School.

Just then, the children returned and were escorted to their classes by the assistant teachers. The volunteers continued their particular task while the tense Clara inched out of the room and retired to the bathroom. Curious workers frequented the bathroom. When Pastor Levi was ready to depart, a student was sent to rescue her from confinement. The remainder of the day was uneventful. Thus, the volunteers felt that they had triumphed, and the first day of Bible School was a great success.

After returning home, Sarah desperately wanted to call Clara and apologize, but after consulting with Tom and some of the other helpers, it was concluded that it might create more havoc. Therefore, Sarah decided to try to forget about it and get a good night's sleep because she had a busy day ahead of her.

On Tuesday morning, more children registered. St. Luke's Vacation Bible School boasted one hundred eighty six students. The volunteers worked with unbridled enthusiasm, and everyone wore smiles of contentment.

All at once the door opened, and who should appear? Clara! She stood against the wall until Sarah could stand it no longer. She went over to her and asked if she would like to help with the attendance sheets. Hesitantly, she followed Sarah as Sarah pulled a chair out as a suggestion for her to sit. Clara apprehensively sat down, and Sarah began to explain the procedure for recording attendance. Soon after she began, a student came to the table and announced, "Mrs. Best, you have a telephone call! Please pick up in the office!"

"Ok! Please tell the person that I'll be right there in a few minutes," Sarah replied, as she looked around for someone to assist Clara. Sue Ann overheard the student and quickly came to Sarah's rescue, "Go on and answer the phone. I will assist Clara." As soon as she sat down, Clara immediately rose from the chair and trod on the heels of Sarah.

Because of her upcoming wedding, Sue Ann was in a state of ecstasy. The euphoria she possessed shielded her from the kind of indignation that Clara had just exhibited. In fact, Clara was probably angry because she had informed Pastor Levi that she did not want him to officiate at her wedding. Sue Ann still had not gotten an ok from Pastor to get a pastor who was nondenominationally affiliated. However, she was prepared to take a firm stand.

Sarah hurried down the hallway because she felt that it was a state of urgency. When she discovered that Clara was behind her, she slacked her pace and dropped back to walk with her. As Sarah looked at Clara, she noticed that her hands were trembling. Compassionate Sarah located the first chair that she could find, and asked Clara to sit while she stooped down beside her. "Do you want to talk about your problem?" Sarah asked.

"No! No! No! I can't, because you wouldn't understand," Clara declared.

Sarah was very curious, but on the other hand she was cautious, so she had to give herself some time to think. She leisurely walked away, and when she reached the first room on the hall, she tiptoed in so as not to disturb the second grade that was in progress. When she had located an empty chair, she dragged it to the hallway beside Clara, sat down and spoke very softy, "Tell me. Maybe, I'll understand."

Sweet Peppers-Sour Grapes & Wild Flowers

Clara whispered, "I'm feeling so-o-o nervous. You see. I had a nervous breakdown some years ago. I think I told you about the young woman that I thought Carl was involved with when we were in Germany. Well, what I didn't tell was that Carl made me feel that I was hallucinating about seeing the girl run pass me. Then, I began to think that I was too. Anyhow, right after that I had a nervous breakdown. Carl was extremely attentive. He didn't leave my side until I had the capability to do for myself."

Still curious about Clara's motive, Sarah asked, "Why would you tell me this at this time?"

Clara looked somewhat confused, "If you would use the material that I planned, it would prove that I am mentally capable of doing something constructive."

"Isn't there something else that you would like to do?" Sarah inquired.

"I can't think of anything. I spent so much time devising the plan for the departmental program. We **should** try for the next three days. It would make a difference. You would just love it, if you would read it. I have another copy that I could give to you. You know I did take some theology courses a few years ago. I thought that Bible School would be a good beginning for me to use my knowledge."

At this point, Sarah had almost discontinued being so ingratiatingly polite, "Mrs. Levi, we have organized our Bible School, and we will not deviate from the plans. Did you tell me your problems because you felt that I would commiserate with you? Yes! I do have sympathy for you, but we can't interrupt our program because you feel that you have something better."

All the while Sarah was in the hallway talking with Clara, members of St. Luke were going back and forth down the hall. They listened very intently, but did not accomplish their mission.

Sarah had missed her telephone call. She inquired about it, and she was told that the person said that she would call back. When she rejoined the group, certain members were very inquisitive about the conversation that she had with Clara. At this point and time, Sarah's answers were guarded and noncommittal.

Following the conversation, Clara scurried to the car and waited for Pastor Levi. It was not very long before Pastor rejoined her, and the two sped off to their destination.

Clara's unfortunate story depressed Sarah. She wondered if Clara would like to continue her recollections. She decided to drop by her house on the way home from Bible School. She drove up into the driveway and came to a halt. As she was egressing from the car, Pastor Levi rushed out of the house with his shirt half out of his pants. His complexion had a flush, and his hair stood upright. When Pastor hustled toward her, she opened the car door and stood with one foot on the ground. Sarah was flabbergasted when he spoke, "Sarah, will you lend me fifty dollars if you have it? I have a presentation to make at the hospital, and I am in charge of the refreshments. I will pay you back soon."

Speechless, Sarah sat back in the car. She pulled her checkbook from her purse and wrote him a check for fifty dollars. Pastor Levi said, "Thank you!" Then he went to his car, got in and drove off. In disbelief, Sarah got back in her car and drove straight to her own home.

Sarah's day had certainly deviated from the norm, and she could not wait to get home and discuss it with Tom. With patience, she waited for Tom to come home. Usually, when he was late, he would call home. It was getting late, and she had not heard from him. She ate a solitary dinner. Then she made a futile attempt to relax by soaking in a bubble bath. Waiting in anguish, she got into bed, but with persistent efforts, she could not sleep. The ticking clock on the nightstand displayed nine o'clock! Then ten o'clock! Then eleven o'clock! About fifteen minutes later, Sarah heard a key in the front door, and Tom whistled as usual as he entered. When it was confirmed that he was alive and well, Sarah displayed her outrage. "You don't know how to telephone home anymore if you are going to be late? I have been so worried that I could barely eat, and as you see I am not sleeping and ...."

Refusing to let Sarah continue, Tom interrupted, "I had an emergency meeting. As I rushed out of the office, I asked my secretary to call you and inform you that I would be home late. Maybe around eleven."

"Oh! That must have been your secretary that called me when I was delayed. I got to the office too late to receive the call," Sarah replied.

With an expression of regret on his face, Tom apologized, "I am sorry that you have gone through so much. Maybe, I should have called myself. Did she leave her name so that you could have returned the call?"

Feeling a little silly for sounding so unpleasant, Sarah said, "I guess it was my fault. I should have gone straight to the office. Anyway, how was your day?"

"Full of frustrations on top of frustrations," Tom exclaimed as he shook his head. "How was your day?"

"We will share our frustrations some other time. It's getting late. Let's go to bed," Sarah said as she yawned.

As Tom undressed and rushed into the bathroom, he called back, "I'm going to take a quick shower, and I'll be right there!"

When he returned to the bedroom, Sarah was fast asleep. He crawled in beside her, and in a few minutes, he too was sound asleep.

Wednesday, the third day of Bible School was a scorcher. The church volunteers did not mind the heat. Some were dedicated, whereas, others were curious. They had heard about Clara's two mysterious visits, and they were not about to miss the third one. Everyone anticipated Clara's grand entrance, but no such thing happened. At the end of the day, the workers gathered to collaborate on accomplishments and suggestions for improvements. The day was a successful, uneventful day.

The fourth day of Bible School, more students enrolled. The attendance soared up to two hundred ten students. Teachers were engaged in making preparations for the culmination activities for Friday. Thus a celebration would take place on the last day of Bible School. At the end of the day, newsletters and invitations were available for the students to take home to their parents.

On Friday morning the festive celebration began at nine o'clock. Many students registered the last day just to be able to join the merriment. Inside in the sanctuary, parents and relatives flocked to observe the culmination performance. Sarah and Kathy stood at the door to greet the parents, relatives and friends. Clara sauntered in and passed by Sarah as she looked straight ahead without speaking. Finding her usual spot in a corner, she sat uncommunicative. She attended to observe Kirk perform because Kate was too obstinate to take part.

On the church grounds, the men were barbequing chicken, hamburgers and hot dogs. There were many other dishes to supplement the meats.

After the presentation in the sanctuary, the crowd was dismissed for the balloon launch. A prayer was delivered before the colorful balloons, with a Biblical Scripture within, floated into the clear blue sky. Immediately, the students forged ahead to the picnic grounds.

For Sarah, this day represented the conclusion of a job well done with members of the group sharing adequately. The program was **extraordinary.** The students' performance was **exceptional**. On the picnic grounds, Sarah mingled with the guests as she welcomed the compliments that they showered upon her. She possessed a real sense of self-satisfaction. Turning to leave the grounds, she observed Clara sitting in the car waiting for Pastor and the twins. Just as she had made up her mind to go to the car and force her to talk, Pastor Levi and the twins got in the car, and they drove off.

On Sunday morning, the St. Luke's volunteers were still full of exhilaration from the delightful week of Bible School. As the people entered the door, an usher handed them a bulletin. Each bulletin contained an insert of a letter from Pastor Levi. The unexpected letter read as follows:

Dear Members of St. Luke,

You will probably have a vacancy after the end of the month. I have made my name available on the call list. It appears that my presence here at St. Luke has impeded its progress and provided for incessant conflict. My wife and I have decided to move on. My children don't seem to be adjusting very well.

It is difficult for me to apply my theological training and some basics of the doctrine to the theological climate of St. Luke because you possess the uppermost characteristics of a dysfunctional organization.

For some unknown reason, the parish administration has been composed of elaborately interconnected parts. Therefore, it seems to be confusing and impossible to implement. I have tried in many ways to energize you, but I was unsuccessful.

Personal factors have influenced my decision. An active church member that you know has been making harassing calls, causing my wife and children to be fearful. My children get hysterical every time the phone rings. The phone company has disregarded my plea. I am afraid that the police apathy could put us in more danger. We have also received death threats. We reported it, but the police are not sympathetic to our concerns, for they see no need for any action.

The amount of money that I am receiving is not enough for me to support my family. All the above and other stressful situations have put a strain on my marriage. So, 'God Bless!'

Sincerely,

Pastor Carl Levi

This Sunday in July marked the doomsday at St. Luke. As Sarah and Tom sat almost in the front pew, Sarah held the letter and read it over and over. It seemed that the words appeared to be so harsh and insensitive. The words incapacitated her mind. They clogged her ears. All the sounds in the church were perceived as rhythmical beats. Inattentiveness engulfed her as she finally became cognizant of the fact that this was a revengeful letter from a pastor that had no compassion for his members.

When the service was over, the ushers directed the members to proceed to the rear row by row as usual. As they walked out, their faces bore a resemblance of a funeral march.

As Tom and Sarah rode home, Sarah said, "I feel like there has been a death. What's your thought about the letter?"

Tom tried to explain his feelings, and at first, he found them inexplicable. Then he gave the matter careful thought and stated, "If that's his decision, or excuses or whatever, so be it."

Sometimes Tom's answers could be so perplexing to Sarah. She became anxious to talk with one of the church ladies.

As soon as Sarah reached home, she dropped her purse on the chair and reached for the telephone. She thought that discussing the letter with another member might help her to understand the nature of the letter. She dialed Holly's number. The telephone rang and rang. No one answered, so Sarah hung up. It then occurred to her that the members that would be interested in collaborating about the letter had remained for Sunday School. "Returning to Sunday School would be a great idea," she thought. Taking expeditious action, she rushed out the door, jumped in the car, and was at church in no time. When she reached the room, the discussion of the bible lesson was underway. This was exactly what Sarah needed. The consecrated discussions and the jubilant people gave Sarah much contentment.

Afterward some of the members gave their opinion about the letter. General opinion was that, in the letter, Pastor Levi declared that the congregation was dysfunctional, in spite of his inefficaciousness. This letter clearly indicated that he was vindictive and ruthless. For Sarah, it was comforting to know that her feelings were not exclusive.

Chapter XVI

The Wedding

Across Kingston, Virginia, people were buzzing about the upcoming wedding. Sue Ann Smith and Sammy Jones were getting married on Saturday. Sue Ann was well known because of her prominence in the banking business. Her amiable personality was a desirable attribute for her occupation. Many customers would postpone their appointments to obtain Miss Smith's assistance.

When it came to personal business, she was dauntless but somewhat diplomatic in her attack. She was aware that Sammy was apprehensive when it came to upholding his belief. He possessed the "desire to please" disease. As far as Sue Ann was concerned, it was not a disease, for it would be a benefit to their marriage.

Sammy, the factotum, was **the** maintenance man. It seemed that there was nothing that he could not fix. He was known as the fix-it man throughout the town. Landscaping was his hobby, for it gave him great self-satisfaction. It was stimulating for him to take a spot that was displeasing in appearance and make it resplendent. He was aware that Hue was delighted over the transformation of his yard since he had become his gardener. However, Sammy sensed Hue's behavior as a little suspicious. It was peculiar that he had not seen any more liquor bottles since he consulted Hue's opinion about them. Besides, he detested Pastor Levi's presence while he labored in the yard. When he was observing him, his sweat glands seemed to have exuded more moisture. Regardless, the gratification of the job and the generous salary he received gave him the fortitude to continue. He admired Sue Ann's courageousness to stand up to Pastor Levi. At least, he would not have to stand before him on the day of the wedding.

Sarah and Holly were engaged in trying to squeeze in the bridal shower before the wedding. It was scheduled for Tuesday evening at Sarah's residence. Invitations were sent out a week earlier. Other miscellaneous tasks had to be performed. Decorating, preparing food, and obtaining games necessitated some time and energy; however, the jovial group of ladies found it relaxing and enjoyable. They were elated, and they rejoiced. The excitement of a wedding had put splendor in the air and exuded triumph at St. Luke.

On Tuesday, Sarah and the hostesses graciously welcomed the guests. The family room was filled to capacity. Exhilaration permeated the room as the group participated in the games. The food! Everyone wanted to know- "Who made this? And who made that? Oh! That was delicious! What a delectable dish!" For Sue Ann, the unfathomable was real, and it was intoxicating as she gazed at the gorgeous gifts. As her excited fingers tore away at the coverings, household items and personal articles emerged from the beautiful wrappings.

Standing before the group at the end of the evening with misty eyes, Sue Ann whimpered as she spoke, "I honestly can't say what it means to me to have people surrounding me that are so gracious! So generous! So –so! Oh! How I love you all! I thank all of you from the bottom of my heart!" Hugs, kisses and handshakes were some of the parting renditions as the guests departed.

Rehearsal on Friday evening was next on the agenda. Indeed, who could ever imagine, St. Luke parishioners being so full of optimism and happiness as they concluded the evening with the clean-up crew. All of a sudden, it hit Sarah, "Clara didn't show up this evening!"

Holly chuckled, "Didn't you notice that we had a jubilant evening?"

Sue Ann squealed, "We did! We sure did!"

"Well, we did not have that nincompoop here to put a damper on our evening. Anyway, Sarah, she would have spent the evening following you around, " Holly said as she observed the compassionate Sarah. Then she said, "Sarah, cheer up. Clara didn't care to socialize with us. Don't you realize that?"

Looking somewhat dejected, Sarah began to explain, "I know. I just wish we all could be happy together. But, I'll forget it, and we'll see each other Friday night for rehearsal."

On Friday night, Pastor Levi hurried to the church to insist on directing the rehearsal. As the wedding party entered the church, he walked toward them and asked, "Are we ready for rehearsal?"

His persistent efforts annoyed Sue Ann, and she did not hesitate to make it known. Straightforward, she said, "Yes, we are ready, but we are waiting for Reverend Jukes. He has to rehearse with us tonight, so that he will be ready for tomorrow."

With an authoritative voice, Pastor Levi announced, "That man you call Reverend Jukes is not denominationally affiliated, and he will not be allowed in this church."

By this time, Sammy was whispering to Sue Ann, but she did not listen, she looked at Pastor Levi and asked, "Is that an authoritative order from the district or is it a personal request?"

With his voice quivering, he stated, "It is a personal request from...."

Rev. Jukes entered and interrupted with his friendly deep voice, "Good evening, folks!" He wore a broad smile as he walked over, extended his hand to Pastor Levi and gave him a firm handshake. As usual, Pastor Levi reciprocated with a weak handshake. As he released his hand, he continued speaking with his amazingly resonant voice, "Pastor Levi, it is so wonderful to see you again! Thank you so much for inviting me over once more! When Sue Ann asked me to officiate, I rearranged my schedule to accommodate her. I have known her and Mr. Jones for such a long time."

Now Pastor Levi was not sure if this Reverend was unaware of the problems at St. Luke, but just for tonight, he would harmonize with him. For some unknown reason, he felt very uncomfortable in his presence. So he decided to sit and size him up before he departed.

Rev. Jukes turned to the group and said, "How are you all doing?"

By now, most of the people were chitchatting. Those that were listening intoned, "Fine! Thank you!"

Nellie started the music and the wedding director began the rehearsal. After a few hours of practice, it seemed that everyone was refined to the point of readiness. At this point everyone was ravenous for food. The next stop was the rehearsal dinner at Crème De La Crème Café where Sue Ann presented the wedding participants with gifts. It was an evening of good food, good fun and lots of laughter.

Saturday was a gorgeous day for a wedding. There was not a cloud in the beautiful blue sky. After all the savvy, extraordinary work and the refined practicing, what could go wrong?

Sue Ann and the bridal party arrived at the church ahead of time, allowing time to put the finishing touches on and begin the wedding promptly. To her amazement, the church doors were locked, and the early guests were standing around outside under shade trees. Others remained in their cars. Before Sue Ann could think, she exploded, "What in the hell has happened?"

Nellie had just arrived and was exiting from her car, when she observed the beautiful bride perturbed and was about to handle the locked doors' situation. Immediately, she interceded, "I'll handle this! Just sit back and stay cool." That instant, she spotted Tom driving on the church's parking lot. Nellie hastened to Tom's car before he could exit. Being demonstrative with her hands, she proclaimed, "Hope you have your keys! The church doors are locked! Hurry along! Open the doors!"

Tom exclaimed, "Oh my God! I don't have my keys. I left them at home because I didn't want to have a bulging pocket. Joe came over earlier and unlocked the doors. I wonder…"

"Do something! We want to keep the bride calm!" Nellie shouted.

"I'll just go back home and get my keys." Wasting no time, he sped off the church grounds and was on his way home.

Nellie and Holly attempted to keep the bride calm while they concocted an excellent excuse for the locked doors. Thereby, they mingled with the waiting guests with smiling expressions while they expressed their sympathy for the emergency that befell the person that was assigned to unlocking the doors. After that they milled around talking small talk, when suddenly, Tom was back. He came to a quick halt, jumped out of his car and hastened to open the doors.

As the guess entered the church, Holly noticed that the bows and ribbons had been removed from the aisle seats. "Thank God!" She said aloud as she retrieved them from the floor. "At least the villain left them at church." Some of the people that assisted Holly in replacing them were unidentified guests. Holly thanked each one repeatedly.

The wedding was running a few minutes behind, but everything seemed to have been shaping up when Pastor Levi came strolling in with wrinkled shorts and t-shirt with his Bible in his hand.

Holly surmised that it was expedient that she immediately inform Sue Ann of Pastor Levi's attire. Rushing to the room where the wedding party was dressing, Holly twisted her foot, and piercing pains shot through her right ankle. Hobbling to the room and quietly opening the door, she limped over to Sue Ann and whispered, "Pastor Levi is wearing unsightly shorts and t-shirt. Don't become upset. We'll just pretend that he is invisible."

Observing the tension on Holly's face, Sue Ann disregarded what Holly was saying, and she exclaimed, "Good heavens! Are you ok?"

"Sure! Sure!" Holly declared, as she stood erect so that Sue Ann would not detect the deception. When Sue Ann turned to retrieve an item, Holly hobbled to the kitchen and iced her ankle. With an earnest and strenuous attempt, she made her way to the sanctuary and sat on the back row. She was fully aware that under the present circumstances, her service was terminated.

At this time, the intonation of the music indicated that it was time for the ceremony to begin. Reverend Jukes made his move and stood at the front of the church. In his grotesque outfit, Pastor Levi appeared from his corner in the pulpit and stood beside him.

Tom went around the back way, came in the side door, came up from behind Pastor and whispered in his ear. He and Pastor quietly moved to the first exit door while Reverend Jukes began the wedding ceremony.

Tom proceeded to the robe rack with Pastor trailing in tow. Being very furious with the vindictive pastor, it took tenacity to speak with reverence. He ground his teeth and bridled his tongue as he said, "We don't mind your being a part of the wedding, but you must put on a robe. Then the only deviance would be those rusty shoes." As he spoke, he selected the white robe, pulled it from the rack and assisted Pastor into it. With no resistance he slipped into the robe.

Without uttering a word, Pastor quietly tiptoed back to the sanctuary. Unexpectedly, Pastor Levi strolled to the corner of the pulpit and sat as if he were in a control booth.

Tom exited the back way and rejoined the ushers. The wedding was underway. All of the groomsmen were in place, and the bridesmaids were proceeding down the aisle. Then the ring bearer followed. Behind him was the flower girl sauntering along dropping rose petals. The time came for Mr. Smith, Sue Ann's uncle, to escort her down the aisle. In the state of euphoria, Sue Ann latched on to Mr. Smith's arm. She wore a white satin gown with a lace bodice, long sleeves, basque waist with an a-line skirt and cathedral train. She carried a bouquet of roses and stephanotis. When she reached the altar, Sue Ann Smith and Sammy Jones exchanged wedding vows without another mishap.

Directly following the wedding was the reception. Attending the reception was out of the question for Holly. Her ankle had swollen, so she decided to seek medical assistance.

Guests poured into the banquet hall. During the dinnertime, Sue Ann observed Pastor Levi and Clara entering the door. Pastor had changed into a frumpy suit. However, Clara was as fashionable as always. They found a seat at a table where there were no St. Luke members. When they completed their dinner, they suddenly departed.

The reception went as planned, and as the night came to a conclusion, guest departed, and Mr. & Mrs. Sammy Jones were off to a secret place for the night. They planned a trip to St. Lucia, British Virgin Islands in the fall.

Chapter XVII

Scrutiny of the Situation

Yes! This was another Sunday morning that the customary service was bestowed upon St. Luke members. The joyful festive celebration, that took place on the day before this day, was just a memory. Most of the parishioners took a walk down memory lane while Pastor Levi presented his usual boring sermon. Once again, the members looked forward to Sunday School where Joe and Sammy would bring the Bible to life. Sunday School was an affirmation that St. Luke was inextinguishable. It was informative and consecrative. The participants departed with jubilation and a desire to search the scripture for more knowledge.

The following week, the Board of Directors attended their scheduled meeting with Pastor Elbert. Everyone arrived on time with the exception of Pastor Levi and Dr. Dawson. The group waited for fifteen minutes, then Tom called the meeting to order. The meeting proceeded headlong in the proper order. When it was time for old business, Pastor Elbert was hesitant to discuss the outcome of the survey when Pastor Levi was not present. At the end of the meeting, Pastor Elbert began to give the summary of the survey. He stated, "According to the survey…"

Just then, Pastor Carl Levi and Dr. Hue Dawson entered the room. It was certain that they had concocted something. Pastor Elbert waited for them to find a seat, and then he started anew, "Now that Pastor Levi is here, I will give you a brief summary of the survey. According to the survey, the parishioners rated Pastor Levi as very poor in all areas. However, the problem seems to be working itself out in that Pastor Levi has put his name on the call list. I will read some of the comments, if you wish to hear them."

A couple of the members stated, "Please do!"

As Pastor Elbert read the list of comments that he had copied in his notebook, Pastor Levi sat gazing at the floor.

When Pastor Elbert finished, Hue Dawson raised his hand, and the chair recognized him. He stated, "Mr. Chairman, now that Pastor Elbert has finished his list, I would like to read a list of maltreatments that have been directed toward the Pastor's wife. Rummaging through the pockets of his white doctor's jacket, he pulled out all kinds of medical pamphlets, but he couldn't seem to find the one paper that he desired. This was truly a test of self-discipline for the board members. Each one squashed his counter-arguments.

Hue started muttering to himself, "Just a minute? I **know** I had that sheet! It should have been right here in my pocket. What happened to it, I don't know." Then he discontinued his muttering and began to talk to the group. "Well, anyway, I will say –The St. Luke members do not communicate with Clara. They even shun her. She faces much hostility from the ladies of the church. Just the other day, one of the ladies snatched her Bible School plans, ripped them up and threw them in the trashcan. Now, let- me -see. What else was on that list, Carl?"

Looking in another direction, Pastor Levi completely and altogether ignored Hue's question. The board members could tell that Pastor Levi did not want to be a spokesman because he was looking downright sneaky. He had prompted Hue to address this matter. On the other hand, he had not properly prepared him.

Pastor Elbert and all the board members remained silent while waiting for Hue to proceed with the list. Some of the members were anxious, and some were angry.

Looking somewhat frustrated, Hue digressed, "Also, I would like to cite some instances of child abuse to the twins. Kate and Kirk do not like to attend church or Sunday School because of the insults they confront. When children have to deal with unfavorable comments each time they are present, they will dislike the place. Children are our future, and we should treat them with respect."

By this time, everyone was staring at Hue with the exception of Tom. He pretended that he was not listening to what he considered nonsense. No matter how he tried to playact, repressed anger was building up in him as he heard Hue say, "I just think that we should be careful how we treat the Pastor's wife and kids."

Hue's remarks exasperated Tom to the point that he said, **"Meeting is adjourned!"** Then he hastened out the door to avoid talking to Pastor Levi. Once he was outside, he took a deep breath.

Sweet Peppers-Sour Grapes & Wild Flowers

The fresh air rendered some serenity. As he was entering his car, Sue Ann was standing on the side of her car that was parked next to his.

Sue Ann asked, "Where did all those lies come from? Who has mistreated his wife and children?"

Tom took a deep breath. Then he spoke, "Doggone it! I am furious! Everyone has given their **all** to accommodate Clara, Kate and Kirk. I guess it is as Sarah said – '**they are just downright unappreciative!**"

Sue Ann moved closer to Tom and whispered, "I acknowledge that Holly put Clara's work in the trashcan, but she didn't snatch them. She retrieved them from the desk. All of us sanctioned that act because we were sick and tired of Clara's trying to interrupt the Bible School. Holly only did that because Sarah has such an ice cream heart that she was afraid that Sarah might succumb to Clara's wishes. You know that would have been devastating for our Bible School."

Then Tom asked, "Who has mistreated those kids?"

"To my knowledge, no one has mistreated them," Sue Ann recounted. "We bent over backward in Bible School with Kate and her nasty attitude. I was glad that she was under the supervision of Mrs. Cole because I don't think I would have put up with her. Clara should have given **all of us** an award and especially Mrs. Cole. Now--- he might have been referring to the time back in March when we were determined to get Kate to say, 'Thanks for the birthday party'. Kirk seemed to have accepted the reminder and was delighted to express his 'Thanks'. Other than that we have been more than kind to them."

"Boy, oh boy! They are wearing my…Bye! Talk to you later!" Tom said as he quickly got into his car. Pastor Levi was exiting the church with Pastor Elbert on one side and Dr. Dawson on the other side. He did not have a desire to talk to any of them. He knew that he would not be a wholesome conversationalist. As they started toward his car, Tom drove off as if he were not aware of their intentions.

Pastor Elbert's church was located in Oxford, Virginia; therefore, it took Tom a while to drive home. During his drive, he reflected on the allegations that Hue had made. It was evident that Pastor Levi was the instigator because Hue was an infrequent attendee at church.

Furthermore, he had been absent for the last two months. It seemed that Pastor Levi was prevaricating more and more these days.

Tom was so lost in thought that he passed his driveway. Returning to his driveway, he drove the car into the garage and exited from it. Inside the house he dialed Sue Ann. There was an urgent desire to continue discussing the allegations that were made at the meeting.

Sue Ann Smith quickly picked up the phone. She was anticipating a call from Mr. Best, as she called him. "Hello!"

"Hi! Ms. Smith! Excuse me! I mean Mrs. Jones! I was hoping that you had gotten home. You know, I still can't get over the idea of Hue's accusations. Why- we haven't seen him at church for months. How does he know what is going on at church?"

Sue Ann emphatically answered, "He doesn't know what is going on. He is listening to what Pastor Levi tells him. Pastor Levi only tells him what he wants him to know. As for me, I am so disgusted with the **entire** Levi family. We gave the twins a birthday party, and the parents didn't have the decency to say 'thanks' in spoken or written form. I stayed on their butts and threatened to send notes myself if they didn't. After weeks Clara passed envelopes up and across church during service. That was done because she didn't wish to fraternize with the members. I wonder what happened if the person did not attend church that Sunday. Likewise, they did not respond in any way when she had surgery. We were kind enough to visit her, wash, cook, clean and buy groceries. They never said a mumbling word to any of us. What else could we have done?"

By now Tom had leaned back in the chair and was listening attentively. When he got a chance to speak, he said, "I don't know how long I can take this. He is still using my old car. Sarah and I don't need it, but he should show some sign that he intends to purchase his own."

Sue Ann continued, "We know that Clara is mentally weak, but that's no excuse for the allegations."

Tom and Sue Ann discussed the situation for a while and then said good-bye. They both realized that the collaboration was very therapeutic for the both of them.

While Tom was on the telephone, Sarah was sitting nearby, waiting attentively for him to finish his conversation on the phone, so that she could let him know that he had a message waiting for him on the voice mail. After Tom hung up, he began to relate some of the happenings to Sarah, whereby she interrupted and said, "Pastor called before you got home. I was not at home, so he left a message on the voice mail."

Tom sat back in a relaxed position and disregarded Sarah's comment.

Sarah repeated, "Tom, Pastor Levi called while we were out. He left a message for you. Aren't you going to listen to it? It appeared that there is some urgency."

Reluctantly, Tom picked up the phone and listened to Pastor's mumbling, "Mr. Best, this is Pastor Carl Levi. I guess you think that I put Dr. Hue Dawson up to those remarks, but I didn't. We'll have to talk as soon as you get in. So if you have time, call me and we can discuss tonight's meeting. Sometimes things go disarray when we try to do the best that we can. I want to make the best of everything. You might think that I am playing the two ends against the middle. But that is not true. I am trying to accomplish certain goals in the way it should be done. I hope that you understand. Anyway, call me when you get in. There are other matters that we should discuss. We don't want to wait too long to settle a matter. These matters should be settled and out of the way. Anyway, I guess that is it. We can talk further. Good night," he said in a monotone voice.

Placing the receiver on its cradle, Tom shook his head as he said to Sarah, "Pastor is lying! He knows that he put Dr. Dawson up to that. How would Hue have known about it? My guess is that they came in late because Pastor wanted to wait for Hue so that he could read the allegations. He seems to be playing me for a fool now, and I don't like it!"

Now Sarah had instant sympathy for Pastor Levi. It seemed that he had struck out. Pastor definitely needed Tom in his corner. Also, Tom's guidance was a necessity for his survival at St. Luke. According to the gibber jabber on the voice mail, no doubt, Pastor Carl Levi realized that Mr. Tom Best's concern was indispensable.

The next day, Tom and Sarah left town for their summer home in the mountains of Pennsylvania. During their interlude, they would be visiting with relatives and friends. Tom did not respond to Pastor Levi's call before leaving. Vacationing away from Kingston was a welcome respite from mediating, negotiating, intervening and doing whatever was necessary to keep things going.

The board members thought that the preposterous allegations necessitated a meeting. So the group decided to meet and collaborate. The night that they congregated to collaborate, Tom was out of town, so Sue Ann, the vice-president presided. This was not an official business meeting; therefore, a quorum was not required. Non-board members were accepted with pleasure. James Holland attended; even though, he was not a board member. Pure and simple, they met to discuss means that they could use to legally rid St. Luke of Pastor Levi. Sue Ann shared some of the items that she and Tom had discussed the night of the meeting. How therapeutic it was for the attendees to regurgitate what had been done; what should have been done; and most of all, what they were going to do.

Dr. Hue Dawson did not attend the meeting, but he apprised Pastor Levi about the meeting. With Tom being out of town, Pastor did not rely on anyone to work in an advisory capacity for him. Thus, he did not give the matter careful thought. He immediately called the four board members that attended the meeting and informed them that they would be disciplined. They would not be allowed to partake of communion at St. Luke until further notice.

The following Sunday was Holy Communion Sunday. For an extended time, Mrs. Jean Palmer had been confined to her home. She was aware that St. Luke had installed a new pastor; however, he had not visited her to administer the Lord's Supper. The elderly lady came to a definitely and earnest decision that she would have to visit church in order to participate in Holy Communion. Since she had been ailing over an extended period of time, she needed some presentable clothing to wear. Some friends assisted her with that matter. Her son, Luther, owned a truck, and the ascension into the truck was going to be difficult for a partially handicapped person. So he graciously rented a car for Sunday. The visit to church was costly and inconvenient, but everyone involved felt that it would be worth it when Mrs. Palmer receives the Holy Communion.

On the following Sunday, the service proceeded in the usual order until the distribution of the communion. Two of the members that had been put on pastoral discipline proceeded to the communion table.

Instantly, Pastor discontinued serving the bread while his helper stood holding the chalice. He immediately covered the supper. Then he recited the closing liturgy while poor Mrs. Palmer sat waiting to be granted communion. The group of members, who waited in line to be served, whirled around and marched back passing by the place where they had been seated as they paraded out the door. Some of them had no intentions of returning again.

Mrs. Palmer's son, Luther, had many obligations at his church, so that prevented him from attending St. Luke with his mother. When he returned from his church to assist Mrs. Palmer out of church, she downheartedly expressed how she was rejected, "The preacher, whom I have never met, ignored me. He stopped the communion for some reason. He covered it up and closed church. I looked around and saw some people leaving church. Had I known that there was some kind of confusion here, I would not have gone through all this trouble to get here."

With sympathy for his mother, Luther replied, "Mother, I have suggested over and over that you let me invite Rev. Jukes over to the house to give you bread and wine."

Gently speaking and with tears in her eyes, Mrs. Palmer uttered, "Honey, I would like to receive communion from my **own** church. I have been attending this church for forty years. I was in the old church with Pastor Trombone. Oh! Those were the '*Good old days*!"

Misty-eyed Luther asked, "May we go Mother?" But, as he looked around, he discovered several members waiting to talk to his mother. So he stood back, as he heard apologies and promises to come by the house to explain it all to her. Some hugged and kissed her, and others gave her a gentle touch on the shoulder.

Luther realized that it would take a lot of encouragement from many of the parishioners to mentally stabilize his mother after what she had witnessed today. Like most elders, she was inflexible and would not consider communion from any other church. Maybe now she would have a change of heart.

Pastor had the audacity to take his usual station at the door. Most of the members went by him as if he were invisible. Luther did not try to hide his disgust as he ushered Mrs. Palmer by him. Pastor Levi stood alone with no support system. For it was rumor that Clara was attending another church.

Holly was on crutches, but she was curious. She limped over and shook Pastor's lifeless hand, and she inquired, "Where is Clara? I have not seen her for quite some time."

With a somber tone, he answered, "Clara is attending another church."

Holly walked away without saying another word.

During the next week, from Holly's observation, Pastor Levi was very busy each day working on the computer. She became suspicious and was inclined to discover why he was so engrossed in the material. Pretending to borrow a colored pencil from the computer desk, Holly hobbled around and peeked over his shoulder to get a glimpse. It appeared that he was composing a letter to the congregation. She caught sight of, *"Dear St. Luke Members."* It seemed that it was Pastor's intentions to keep this letter a secret until presentation. Holly yearned to call Sarah and Tom about the upcoming letter, but they were on a restful vacation and should not be disturbed. Yet, she debated the situation in her mind, and then she thought it might be expedient to call Sue Ann. After all Sue Ann was the next in line on the board and was also in proximity at the present time.

Sue Ann was still employed at the Virginia State Bank. She seemed to have been wearing a smile of contentment since she and Sammy had gotten married. Holly picked up the receiver and dialed. The voice on the other end stated, "Good Morning! This is Virginia State Bank."

In a subdued voice so that Pastor could not overhear her, she asked, "May I speak to Mrs. Sue Ann Smith-Jones?"

The person on the other end announced, "I am sorry, but Mrs. Jones is with a customer. Would you like to have her call you back?"

Still speaking in a soft hushed voice, Holly stated, "No. I'll call her back later. Thank you." Then Holly gently replaced the phone on the hook.

Holly felt that it was pertinent that she informed one of the other board members since she could not reach Sue Ann. She considered calling Sammy, but she knew that she could impart the circumstance to him tonight when he was more relaxed. She pondered the idea for a few minutes, and then she dialed Joe Truss's number. After the telephone rang three times, his secretary answered, "Hello! May I help you?"

Being very careful that she was not heard, she said, "Hello, Nancy!"

Straining to hear, Nancy said, "Hello! Hello! Hello! I can barely hear you!"

Raising her voice a mite, Holly spoke, "Nancy, this is Holly. Is Mr. Truss in?"

Whispering because Holly was whispering, Nancy answered, "Mr. Truss is not in, Holly. He will probably be in later this afternoon. Do you want him to call you at that time?"

"No. You don't even have to mention that I called."

Holly had no doubt that she must contact Sue Ann. She was one of the board members who was on pastoral discipline. At this point she and Pastor Levi were not even speaking to each other. Once again, she called Sue Ann, and this time she answered. She gave Sue Ann an account of the situation based on her observation. At any rate, Sue Ann was very appreciative of Holly's thoughtfulness. She felt that the information was relevant; therefore, she reported it to the other board members.

Pastor Levi seemed to have acquired a sensational amount of power. Now that he had made one decision without Tom's assistance, he felt that he had the capability of greater attainments. He had been communicating with the President of the Virginia District, Pastor Neal Gore and the Circuit Counselor, Pastor John Elbert. Under the present circumstances, he was convinced that he had much information to impart to the congregation.

On the Sunday morning, a gentle summer breeze impeded the sweltering heat. It was a lovely morning! In spite of the difficulties last Sunday, some members returned with perseverance. Also, there was credible hearsay that Pastor Levi would insert another letter in the bulletin this Sunday. Members who had missed the last dubious letter were inclined to obtain this one.

Just before service began, Pastor rushed in and handed his self-prepared bulletins to the ushers. Joe was astonished when he glanced inside, and there was no insert. With skepticism, he and the other usher stood at the door and presented bulletins to each person that entered the church. As Joe observed certain members, he noticed that they took a quick look inside as soon as they received the bulletin. When they glanced back at him with a questionable look, he just executed one of his cynical smiles.

Church service began at nine o'clock with the expected liturgy. When it was time for announcements, Pastor proceeded to the lectern with five sheets of papers, and he commenced to reading. He disclosed the fact that he had been in collaboration with Pastor Neal Gore, President of the District, Pastor Milton Chance, vice-president for the region of the district and Pastor John Elbert the circuit counselor about the unrest at St. Luke. He continued by reading directly from the Constitution and Bylaws starting with the Preamble, and then he read Article I. Reading on, he read Article II, III, IV and V. When he came to Article VI, he began to identify by name the people that indicated reluctance to submit to pastoral admonition. Whereas, he stated, "On July 28th, Kathy Holland impeded the progress of Holy Communion. According to Article VI, Chapter 2, Kathy….."

By this time James Holland was on his feet and he yelled, "You no-good bastard! Don't you insult my daughter before everybody!"

Someone near him said, "Oh, sit down James!" Then he calmly sat down.

For some unknown reason, Pastor felt safe at the lectern. He continued, "Kathy Holland **must** accept her pastoral admonishment!"

That's when all hell broke loose. James sprang from his seat and sprinted down the aisle waving his cane high in the air. There was no noticeable sign of disability. As he ran, he bellowed, "I had intended to forgive you for hurting my toe, but now you are asking for it!"

Holly, who was in the choir loft, grabbed her crutches and lamely descended the stairs. As she stumbled down the aisle, the members were not certain of Holly's intent. Some decided to leave and others stayed for different reasons.

Nellie was sitting at the organ and thought she heard someone say, "He's got a gun!" That instant she leaped from the organ bench. She realized that her dress was caught, but she sensed that she should get out. So as she jerked forward and began to run, her dress ripped completely off her. She left her dress and descended the stairs two by two.

Sue Ann and Sammy were two of the members that were on pastoral discipline. After being informed about the letter, they were afraid that Pastor Levi might harshly rebuke them openly. Seemingly these days, he had assumed the duties of the Omnipotent. It might be a possibility that he would stimulate them to retaliation. They did not wish to be aroused to scandalous behavior. So, all week they had vacillated on whether they would go to church or stay at home. As they arose and peered out the window on Sunday morning, it was so beautiful. Furthermore, they were accustomed to going to church on Sunday morning. So at the last minute, Sue Ann said to Sammy, "You know, Sammy, this is our church. Why should we let some stranger come to town and drive us away?"

Scratching his head while he gave the matter serious thought, Sammy replied, "I think you're right. It seems so odd sitting at home on a Sunday morning. We should fight for our church."

As Sue Ann hurried into the bedroom, she announced, "It shouldn't take me long to get ready!"

There wasn't much time, so Sammy dressed hastily and was sitting on the couch in the living room when Sue Ann came out of the bedroom. Straightaway, they got in the car and sped off to church. When they drove on the church grounds, parishioners were rushing to their cars. Now Sue Ann and Sammy were aware that they were late, but not late enough for church to be concluding. Right then and there, Sue Ann and Sammy spied Nellie scampering across the church grounds on the way to her car wearing only panties and a bra. Even though everything seemed peculiar, they had a hearty laugh at Nellie. As they observed the bustling activity, they pondered on what to do next. Finally Sammy spoke, "Let's go inside and see what's going on."

Seeing all the hurrying and scurrying, Sue Ann had an eerie feeling about entering the church. She moved slowly, and she squinted her eyes as she gave it consideration. Then she uttered, "O-ok! Ma-a-y be."

Upon entering the church, Sue Ann and Sammy observed Pastor Levi ducking and dodging around the pulpit and the lectern. James was behind him swatting at him with his cane. Holly was limping and dragging her crutches along as she tugged at his coat and uttered, "Stop it! Stop it!"

When James was about to catch up with Pastor, Pastor turned and placed the Bible between the two of them, and James gave the Bible a whack. The force caused the Bible to fall to the floor. James stumbled on it, and it impeded his progress. Seeing that he had a little time, Pastor scrambled into his office and locked the door.

Holly attempted to help James to his feet, and she lamely ushered him down the aisle. She was limping on crutches, and James was carrying his cane in a swinging motion while he murmured obscenity under his breath.

The church was nearly empty. As Pastor poked his head out the door to see if the coast was clear, his eyes were as big as saucers and his face was as red as a beet. Of course, he did not see James, so he returned to the pulpit with the upper part of his robe saturated with perspiration. Abandoning his announcements, and with a quivering voice, he restarted the service with the few members that remained. After a tremulous start, he settled down and regained his composure; wherein he endured until the end. Almost at the end, Sue Ann and Sammy tip toed out of church. Since Pastor was not speaking to Sue Ann, she made an effort to steer clear of him.

On her way to the car, Sue Ann shook her head to clear it, as she said, "I can't believe what I have seen today. I **must** be dreaming."

"You saw what you saw. It was for **real!**" Sammy said as he took a deep breath.

The next week, the board called a meeting. Pastor did not attend. Hue Dawson, his representative, read the letter that he sent. The letter read:

Dear Members of St. Luke,

I have met with Pastor Neal Gore, the President of the District, Pastor Milton Chance, Vice-President for the Virginia region of the district, and Pastor John Elbert, our Circuit Counselor. We have thoroughly combed through the constitution and by-laws. It seems that St. Luke is not following the constitution. According to our constitution, Article VIII, paragraph D, women should not serve on the Board of Directors. That makes our board null and void.

Therefore, there is no current board. I will not be meeting with an inauthentic board.

Furthermore, according to Article VII, elections should have been held in March. I assume you were too busy celebrating Black History that you forgot your church duties. Anyway, this year's officers' terms have expired. There is no Board of Directors legally serving St. Luke at this time.

If you insist on meeting to try to remove me, you will receive pastoral admonishment. Anyhow, the process was begun at an illegal call meeting and is not valid by the Virginia District. Any attempt to continue this process shall result in excessively long successions of appeals with church adjudication, hearings and possibly legal action in the court system.

My working with the current Board of Directors has all but terminated. Two members of the Board of Directors have revealed unwillingness to surrender to pastoral admonition. In addition, they impeded the Sunday's Holy Communion. Those members who are now receiving pastoral discipline are Mr. Joe Truss, Mrs. Sue Ann Smith-Jones, Ms. Kathy Holland and Mr. Sammy Jones.

When I, the Pastor, say so, we will call a meeting of the voters' assembly in order that the first order of business will be the election of the Board of Directors. As I see it the voters' assembly meeting will occur sometimes in September after church. Meeting date will be announced later. The church secretary and I will compile a list of all eligible voting members. According to the constitution, you must be eighteen and older, and according to my book, you must have attended at least two services per month this year. We will have a roster available for your signature before you vote.

I will appoint a nominating committee, since there is no Board of Directors. The nominating committee and I will determine the men to appear on the slate. This election will occur in accordance with the by-laws.

On Election Day, I am canceling Sunday school classes. Please be sure that you make arrangements for your children's care. They will not be allowed in the sanctuary where we are voting.

Because of the chaos that certain members induced at the last communion, there will be no communion services celebrated until the unrest in the congregation has ceased. The congregation will not sin against the body of the Lord. We will have a season of prayer.

Mary Flowers Carter

We are also in need of more monetary support in order to carry on our business.

As your pastor, I am here, and I shall see that matters are taken care of according to the constitution and by-laws.

If the congregation wishes to appeal, do so. The address is listed on the back of your Sunday's program.

In Christ,

Pastor Carl Levi

CC: Pastor Neal Gore, Pastor Milton Chance, and Pastor John Elbert

Evidently, Pastor Levi perceived the letter as very important. He made a special trip to the office to inform Holly that it was imperative that she mailed each member a letter.

In Tom's absence, Sue Ann spoke to Pastor Elbert about the letter and the implementation of pastoral admonition; whereby, he indicated that he was in harmony and agreement with Pastor Levi. Now they could understand why Pastor Levi had become so high and mighty and unreasonable. Therefore, the board felt that it was of their best interest to seek further assistance.

The board members composed a letter to Pastor Neal Gore, President of the District, and he directed it back to Pastor Elbert. At this point, the board members were back to square one. They decided to continue to communicate and exchange ideas on how they could get Pastor John Elbert, their Kingston Circuit Counselor to understand.

Chapter XVIII

Strange Appearances

Whatever the answer to St. Luke's problems, the parishioners refused to dwell on them, but they remained vigilant at all times. At this time of the year, the church members gathered to experience the end of the summer picnic. On this excursion, participants donated food, as they look forward to the excitement that they always shared in the open air.

At the entrance of the beach area, there was a sign with an arrow that pointed to shelter "8"-'St. Luke Church'. The afternoon sun radiated on the rooftop, as the church ladies busied themselves around the picnic tables. The men had three barbecue grills in action, and the aroma permeated the area. All around the area were children jumping rope, chasing a ball or playing a board game. A group had even initiated a volleyball game in a shady spot. Sue Ann and Sammy anticipated on playing a tennis match in the cool of the evening.

Of course, this scene clearly demonstrated that a group of faithful members at St. Luke were persistent in their course of action in spite of difficulties.

Just as everyone had begun to eat, there appeared under the shelter an unidentified lady. She was huffing and puffing as she carried a plump baby.

Sue Ann recalled Pastor Daniel Trombone's methods of handling a newcomer who had appeared at his place. He became the most gracious host. With a kind Christian greeting and friendly smile, he accommodated and obliged him in any manner that he possibly could. Desiring to be an exemplary of Pastor Trombone, Sue Ann strolled over and greeted the attractive young lady, "Hello, how are you?"

"I'm fine. I was looking for shelter "8". St. Luke Church!" she stated as she flicked her blond hair from her face.

"This is the place!" Sue Ann proclaimed.

Displaying a warm-hearted smile, Sue Ann asked, "What might be your name? So that I can introduce you to the others."

Flicking her hair again, the blonde answered, "Nina."

Looking at the baby who possessed the bluest of eyes, Sue Ann asked, "And your baby's name?"

"This is Brant." Nina said as she brushed the baby's blonde hair.

As Sue Ann observed Brant, he gave her a broad grin. She smiled back and said, "Hi, Brant! It must be a little warm for you today."

Then Sue Ann began the introduction, "Nellie, Holly, Joe, Sammy- I would like for you to meet Nina and Brant."

Almost in unison, they said, "Hi! Nina and Brant!" And they went about their work.

With an undetectable accent, Nina stated, "I guess I'm ok. It's hot weather!"

Holly interjected, "Would you like some food?" Turning to Sue Ann, she said, "She can meet some of the others later."

"Come right on over and get what you would like," Holly said as she beckoned to Nina to follow her.

As Nina proceeded around the serving table to get some food, she propped the baby on her hip while struggling with her plate. At that point and time, Sue Ann rushed over to assist her. "Would you like for me to hold Brant while you eat," she asked Nina.

"Thank you very much," Nina said as she released the baby. Brant was very pleasant. He smiled and clung to Sue Ann as if she were an acquaintance.

When Nina had completed plenishing her plate, she sat down to dine. Nina, who was featherweight, seemed to have been a very finicky eater. In a dazed condition, she meticulously consumed tiny bits of food. Eating seemed to have been a laborious undertaking for her.

Brant was getting somewhat fussy, so Holly assisted Sue Ann while Nina stared into space and picked at her food. Babysitting was becoming a great responsibility for the two, and Nina did not seem to perceive the significance of reclaiming Brant.

Kathy had been observing the situation while playing Scrabble with the other youths. Finally, she decided that it was high time that she rescued Sue Ann and Holly. She said to the others, "I'll be right back." Then she strolled over to Holly who was rocking Brant and singing, "Hush, Little baby, don't say a word. Mama's going to buy you a mockingbird. If that mockingbird won't sing, mama's going to buy you a diamond ring. If that diamond ring won't shine, mama's going to buy you …"

"May I hold him?" Kathy asked.

"Sure!" Holly extolled Kathy's thoughtfulness, and with great joy she quickly relinquished the baby; even though, Brant was on the verge of sleep. Then, Holly exercised her discomfortable arm. The weight of the baby had numbed it. Sue Ann and Holly were overjoyed that Kathy had extricated them.

Kathy took Brant to the game board, and when she sat, Brant was fully awake and was fascinated with the Scrabble pieces. As he reached for them, Kathy moved backward. The youngsters immediately discontinued the game and began to play with Brant. For a while, so many smiling faces and different voices captivated Brant. But after a while, he became restless and began to whimper. Then finally the whimpering converted to crying.

Under no circumstances did Nina convey any concern. Regardless, Kathy felt it fitting to give Brant to her because she was the mother, and he was becoming unmanageable. She strolled over and handed Brant to Nina. Nina did not seem to be aware of her presence. So Kathy softly uttered, "Nina! Nina! Brant is desirous of something. Do you think he might be hungry?"

Regaining her composure, Nina answered, "He **is** probably hungry." Then Nina took him and caressed him while rubbing his hair down which insisted on standing up. Exhibiting signs of contentment, Brant quietly waited while Nina flipped out her breast and supplied him with nourishment. Wiggling his tiny pink toes, Brant anxiously devoured the content. He was making such a loud smacking noise that many of the guests turned and took a glimpse and quickly looked in another direction. From this incidence, most of the ladies became aware of the fact that Nina was from out–of–town because Kingstonians were a bit more reserved.

While Brant was being pacified, Sue Ann asked, "Are you from around here?"

"No, I'm living in Boston these days. I'm just visiting here for a few days," Nina replied with a lovely smile.

Nellie interjected, "You probably find that it is warmer here."

"Yes, quite-a-bit! Quite a bit warmer," Nina said as she bobbed her head up and down.

By this time, Brant was fast asleep, and he had let go of the pink nipple. Nina carefully restored the content, and then she buttoned her blouse. She gathered her possessions, the contented Brant and said,

"Thanks so much for everything." Then she struggled off down the sidewalk. The inquisitors watched until they observed her getting into a red car and driving off.

A few minutes later, Pastor Levi appeared upon the picnic area. Since Tom was not there for him to follow around, he moved around aimlessly. Many of the parishioners treated him as an invisible being. Sue Ann whispered to Holly, "He has a lot of gumption to come out here."

Holly glanced up, and then she whispered back to Sue Ann, "He has to be somewhat foolhardy to have come. Let me go over and relieve him of some of his anxiety." Holly meandered over to him and asked, "Pastor, would you like some food?"

"Yes, thank you." he said politely as never before.

Holly could not wait to ask about Clara. As she followed Pastor to the serving table to assist him, she spouted out, "Where is Clara and the twins?"

"Oh, they have gone on a vacation back in Philadelphia. They will be there for about a month," Pastor Levi said as he piled his plate as if he had been on a starvation diet.

"A month? School starts in a couple of weeks. Will the twins be back in time for school?" Holly inquired.

Pastor explained, "If they are not back in time for school, they have the ability to catch up. But I'll have to talk to their teachers about the situation."

Following him to an eating spot, Holly continued, "How long have they been gone?"

Pastor swallowed a mouthful of food in order to answer. Holly thought she saw it going down his neck. He cleared his throat as if he were buying time for an answer. "They have been gone all week."

"It must be lonesome," Holly said as she observed him gobbling up his food.

After he gulped down the second can of pop, he replied, "Hue comes home quite often lately."

"Good! Then, you are not alone."

As Pastor scraped every morsel from his plate, he gathered his garbage and eased away from the inquisitive Holly. He deposited each item in its labeled receptacle. Then it looked as if he were sneaking

Sweet Peppers-Sour Grapes & Wild Flowers

off, but everyone was eying him. He got in his borrowed Honda and drove off.

When pastor was out of sight, Holly announced to Nellie that Clara was vacationing. She even teased her about the fact that she was probably wearing some of the clothes that she had bought her.

Nellie acknowledged that she realized some time ago that she would take the loss and stock it up for experience. She even took on a few more piano students. Surprisingly, she didn't seem to be angry anymore.

On Sunday morning, there were fewer people in the sanctuary. Most of the youth had matriculated into colleges and universities. Kathy Holland had decided to spend a year in the culinary arts at a university in Maryland. Again and again St. Luke's parishioners continued to pray and worship, even though Pastor Levi continued to control the Sunday's bulletin with the same humdrumness. This Sunday seemed to have been no different.

Today was the first time that communion had been served since the pastoral disciplined board members had allegedly interfered. It was rumor that Pastor had lifted the admonition and had secretly admitted the four board members back to the communion table. Some participated, and others abstained. Most of them were displeased with the way it was handled. Their request was an open apology at a regular general voters' assembly meeting.

Surprisingly, Joe and his wife, Edna, trekked down the aisle to the communion table. During Pastor Levi's tenure, Joe Truss had been the **most** uncompromising of all of the board members. Why, he was downright ruthless at times. Since he and Edna married for the third time a few weeks ago, he had progressed toward compassion and conciliation. In fact, he had discontinued collaborating with the ousted board members.

Of course, Sue Ann and Sammy were adamant about not partaking of the Lord's Supper **ever** under the direction of Pastor Levi. As they sat and waited for the others to be served, to their astonishment, they observed Nina and Brant advancing to the communion table. They watched as Pastor served Nina her bread, and the assistant followed with the chalice of wine.

Sue Ann whispered to Sammy, "Nina is not a member of our church. That is contradictory to our constitution. I wonder if she has conferred with Pastor."

Sammy whispered back, "Who cares about Nina? We'll **never** take bread and wine under him."

Sue Ann didn't say another word. She knew that she would get the truth from Nina right after church.

After church, Sue Ann immediately went to Nina to ask her about her affiliation with the church. But first, she exclaimed, "Nina! How delighted we are to have you and little Brant visit us today!" As she observed Brant, he was bouncing up and down and smiling as if he recognized her. Giving Brant her undivided attention, she softly said, "Hi, Brant! It's good seeing you again." Brant gave her a broad grin and made a baby talking sound, "Na! Na!"

While holding Brant's tiny hand, Sue Ann asked, "Nina, are you affiliated with our church's denomination?"

With a nod of the head, "Nina said, "Uh-huh! My membership remains in Germany."

Sue Ann continued to play with Brant while she pondered over whether to inquire further. While pondering on what to say next, Nina spoke first. When she spoke, she stunned Sue Ann with the **OVERWHELMING** news: "I am here because I am seeking child support for my baby, Brant. His father is Carl Levi. He fathered him while he was in Germany. Now, he wants to deny him."

Sue Ann sat down with her mouth opened, but words would not emerge. All she could say was, "Uh! Uh! Uh!" Then she commenced to squirming around while trying to properly dismiss herself from Nina. All she could think of was, "Well, Nina, it was nice seeing you. Will we see you next Sunday?"

"I'm not sure," Nina said as her eyes wandered as if she were looking for someone.

"Have a good day! Bye, Bye Brant!" Sue Ann turned toward the rear door, and she noticed that Pastor Levi was not in his customary position for the exit greetings. As she hurried to the car, Sammy was waiting for her. He said, "I hope you didn't quiz the poor lady to the point of driving her away."

"No, no, no!" Sue Ann said. She sat quietly, and not a mumbling word was uttered on the way home. She could feel Sammy's piercing eyes observing her.

Sweet Peppers-Sour Grapes & Wild Flowers

Sue Ann decided to keep mum about what Nina had revealed to her. At least she would refrain from speaking about it until Tom returned. It seemed that he was a person who could properly deal with crisises.

As Sue Ann went about her work the next day, her mind reflected on Nina and Brant. Nina appeared to have a very loving nature. Yet, this lovely person declared that she had been involved with the vindictive Carl Levi. Little Brant was so precious. It seemed that she had become fond of him. Now to discover that they have connections with the Pastor seemed to be unreal.

The next day Tom and Sarah returned to Kingston from their summer home in the mountains of Pennsylvania. Tom had received a copy of the last letter that Pastor Levi had composed. As soon as he was in his place of residence, the parishioners commenced to calling. The period of respite was essential; however, Tom felt that some of the occurrences could have been prevented if he had been present. He knew that they wanted to purge their systems, so Tom and Sarah invited the parishioners over for a backyard barbeque. An invitation was extended to Pastor Levi; whereas, he turned it down with a lame excuse.

The adventures at St. Luke were unreal. Tom and Sarah were receptacles for the members as they vocalized their unusual experiences and exciting undertakings. Some of the members even knew about Nina and Brant. It seemed that Nina did not bridle her tongue when she visited the church.

Profoundly, Tom stated, "At St. Luke, we are like a garden of sweet peppers, sour grapes and wild flowers."

Eager to learn more about what Tom was insinuating, Sue Ann asked, "Could you explain that?"

"Just think about it for a while, Sue Ann," Tom said as he bobbed his head up and down with assurance.

Joe chimed in, "There you go again, Tom! -With your philosophical attitude."

Sue Ann was always eager for knowledge, so she continued her inquiry, "Tom, do you mean…"

Tom cut in, "Sue Ann! That is your homework."

With an educator's point of view, Sarah interjected, "Yes, homework makes one more knowledgeable of the subject. But, right now, you have an on-the-spot job. That is – you must eat up. **Please!** Don't leave this food here with Tom and me. **Please!** Get more barbeque! Baked beans! Cole slaw!" With that announcement, Sarah suspended the seriousness. Everyone laughed, had fun and enjoyed the barbeque cookout.

The next day, Tom spontaneously went by Hue's residence to speak with Pastor Levi. He asked him about Nina and Brant. Pastor denied that the baby was his. He said that Nina was outright lying, and he would prove it.

After that Tom did not linger on that subject. He decided to proceed to the next issue. Having been informed of Clara and the twins' vacation, Tom stated, "So the rest of the family is vacationing in Philadelphia, huh."

"Yes, Clara wanted to visit our folks for a while."

"How long will they be gone?" Tom inquired.

Looking away, Pastor answered, "Oh, about a couple of weeks, I guess."

Now Tom distinctly remembered Holly quoting Pastor as saying that his family would be gone for a month. So he remained silent as he observed Pastor Levi squirming with slight perspiration on his forehead. Allowing Pastor to regain control of his thoughts, Tom was certain that he must inquire about the admonition of the four board members while he was out of town. So he said, "So, there has been a reprimanding of members recently."

In an aloof manner, Pastor Levi declared, "I must abide by the constitution and by-laws."

"Tom proclaimed, "Maybe, we should take a look at the constitution once more."

Since pastor revealed an increasingly reticent manner, Tom did not reveal the fact that he had possession of the last letter he had distributed. Thus, he said, "Good day, Pastor Levi." Subsequently, he vacated the premises.

Hue came home. When Hue mentioned Nina and Brant, Pastor threatened to tell everyone about him. Pastor expounded, "You have only been supportive of me because you did not want anyone to know that you once ran an illegal abortion ring out of your home. I found evidence when I arrived here, and remember, we did make a proposition!"

Right then and there, Hue yelled, "Pack your things and move out of my house!"

With a cunning grin, Pastor Levi announced, "I don't have to pack! I've packed already!"

As Pastor proceeded to get his belongings, Hue stated, "I am aware that Clara and the twins have no intentions of returning. I witnessed them taking all of their belongings with them."

Pastor exclaimed, "Dr. Hue Dawson, you think that you are shrewd, but don't be too sure that your violations are not already disclosed."

Hue held the door open so that he could assist Pastor Levi with his departure. With his meager possessions, Pastor struggled to Tom's Honda, threw them in, then he got in and drove off.

Feeling dubious about Pastor Levi's intentions, Hue observed the Honda until it disappeared out of sight. Then he hustled to the telephone and called Tom.

When the telephone rang, Tom answered, "Hello!"

"Hi! Tom! This is Hue. Pastor Levi just left town in your car!"

"I be doggone! Which way did he go?"

"He's probably heading north on his way to Philadelphia where his family is now located!"

Tom threw the telephone down and called to Sarah, "Pastor Levi has just left town in **my** car. I'm going after him."

Sarah stated, "And he owes me some money!"

With astonishment, Tom yelled, "What? When I catch him, I am going put his butt out of **my** car. He will have to thumb his way to Philadelphia."

Sarah stated, "Tom, there is a prediction of a severe hurricane with strong winds. I can hear the wind outside right now! It will probably get stronger and stronger!"

In a fit of anger, Tom felt that he had the capability of conquering anything. So, he shouted at Sarah, "Oh, I'll catch him before the hurricane gets too rough! Let's go!" He rushed out the door, and Sarah reluctantly trailed behind him.

For a while, the raging wind did not permit Sarah to close her car door. When it was finally closed, Tom drove off in the violent storm.

Epilogue

Sarah and Tom were sitting in the creek after being tossed about by the powerful hurricane. Sarah was about to follow Tom's orders when they noticed a truck from the fire department. "Thank God!" Sarah exclaimed.

"Thank Heaven!" Tom echoed.

The storm had calmed down somewhat as the firemen tossed a rope down in the deep creek, and Sarah was pulled to safety. Secondly, Tom was delivered. A police car waited in the rear of the fire truck. Saturated with grimy filthy water, Tom and Sarah crawled into the police car while trying to hide their faces.

The policeman behind the wheel took a good look at the two stinky people, and said, "Lands sakes! Why this is Mr. and Mrs. Best! What are you two doing out in this storm? Did you listen to the weather report?"

Shaking and shivering from the cool autumn breeze, Tom decided to keep quiet. He never felt so dumb in all of his life. But Officer Doug Cray had been dispatched by the fire department, and for the life of him, he could not understand why two intelligent people would get out in such a violent storm. Again, he asked, "Mr. Tom Best, where were you going?"

With quivering lips, Tom said, "It's a long story. Just a thoughtless act."

Still curious, Officer Cray stated, "I must say, it was a **stupid act!** You are lucky to be in the shape that you are in. In fact you could have lost your lives. But, Mr. Best, Uh, Uh, Uh! Not you! You! Maybe everybody goes crazy every once and a while."

Tom felt that he deserved everything that the Officer dished out. Silence was most imperative at this time. All he wanted Officer Cray to do was to deposit him at his home and forget he ever existed.

When Tom and Sarah were safely inside their home, they said a little prayer. The warm peppermint baths felt so heavenly. Tom informed some of the parishioners that Pastor Levi had disappeared. However, he kept all the details of their adventure as confidential as possible.

About the Author

Mary Flowers Carter retired from the public schools in Gary, Indiana after thirty-seven years of service. After retirement, she taught writing at the Gary Community College and reading at Indiana University Northwest. Carter writes with luminous intensity about accountability in the ecclesiastical profession. It is her anticipation that this novel would serve as inspiration for some and a source of knowledge for others.

Mary Carter and her husband reside in Burlington, North Carolina where she is working on her second novel.

Printed in the United States
1258800001B/316-333